GREEN TIGER'S
ILLUSTRATED BOOK OF
Fairy Tales
12 CLASSIC FAIRY TALES
GREEN TIGER'S ILLUSTRATED BOOK OF
FAIRY TALES

LILIAN
ROWLES

GREEN TIGER'S ILLUSTRATED BOOK OF *Fairy Tales*

GREEN TIGER PRESS
MMVIII

ENDPAPERS • HERMANN VOGEL

HALF TITLE • ILLUSTRATOR UNKNOWN FROM JOHN MARTIN'S BOOK, 1926

FRONTISPIECE • LILIAN ROWLES

FIRST PRINTING PRINTED IN CHINA
ISBN13 978-1-59583-287-0

GREEN TIGER PRESS
A DIVISION OF LAUGHING ELEPHANT

WWW.LAUGHINGELEPHANT.COM

TABLE OF CONTENTS

PREFACE

There is an enormous number of fairy tales, most very old and anonymous, some few of known authorship. This book includes a tiny fraction of this vast resource, and I want here to explain how they were chosen.

Excellence was my first requirement. Shapely stories are not easy to fashion, and most of them fall short of perfection. The ones that come closest to ideal form are the ones that are remembered and retold. This leads to my second criterion – familiarity.

In the realm of fairy tales cream does rise to the top. The stories with the widest appeal are those that are built on themes of universal appeal, and which develop those themes in a graceful and memorable manner. *The Three Bears* is more familiar than *The Three Brothers* because it is a more fully-realized story. In searching the library in preparation for this volume, I found the same few stories in book after book. These were the ones I wanted.

The final criterion was excellent illustration. We offer here a single illustrator for each story. Most illustrators seemed, to us, to relish the challenge of a story as familiar as *Sleeping Beauty* or *The Ugly Duckling*. Rather than the boredom or world-weariness one might expect in the face of yet another scene of *Cinderella* trying on the glass slipper, or Beauty dining with the Beast, the artists contained herein each depict their subjects with power and authority.

There are lots of other excellent fairy tales. Those included are my preferences from among a small body of wonderful and essential tales. Choosing from the great illustrators in our collection was a difficult task; I chose ones that seemed to capture each tale's spirit. I do hope you will enjoy my selection.

–Harold Darling

H·M·BROCK

Puss-in-Boots

here was once a Miller, who, at his death, had nothing to leave to his three sons except his mill, his donkey, and his cat. The eldest son took the mill, the second took the donkey—and as for the youngest, all that remained for him was the cat.

The youngest son grumbled at this. "My brothers," said he, "will be able to earn an honest living, but when I have sold my cat I shall die of hunger."

The Cat, who was sitting beside him, overheard this. "Nay, Master," he said, "don't take such a gloomy view of things. If you will get me a pair of boots made so that I can walk through the brambles without hurting my feet, and give me a bag, you shall soon see what I am worth."

The Cat's master was so surprised to hear his Cat talking, that he at once got him what he wanted. The Cat drew on the boots and slung the bag 'round his neck and set off for a rabbit warren. When he got there he filled his bag with bran and lettuces, and stretching himself out beside it as if dead, waited until some young rabbit should be tempted into the bag. This happened very soon. A fat, thoughtless rabbit went in headlong, and the Cat at once jumped up and pulled the strings.

Puss was very proud of his success, and, going to the King's palace, he asked to speak to the King. When he was shown into the King's presence he bowed respectfully, and, laying the rabbit down before the throne, he said— "Sire, here is a rabbit, which my master, the Marquis of Carabas, desires me to present to your Majesty."

"Tell your master," said the King, "that I accept his present, and am very much obliged to him." A few days later, the Cat went and hid himself in a cornfield and laid his bag open as before. This time two splendid partridges were lured into the trap, and these also he took to the palace and presented to the King from the Marquis of Carabas. The King was very pleased with this gift, and ordered the messenger of the Marquis of Carabas to be handsomely rewarded.

H·M·BROCK

For two or three months the Cat went on in this way, carrying game every day to the Palace, and saying it was sent by the Marquis of Carabas. At last the Cat happened to hear that the King was going to take a drive on the banks of the river with his daughter, the most beautiful Princess in the world. He at once went to his master.

"Master," said he, "if you follow my advice, your fortune will be made. Go and bathe in the river at a place I shall show you, and I will do the rest."

"Very well," said the Miller's son, and he did as the Cat told him.

When he was in the water, the Cat took away his clothes and hid them, and then ran to the road, just as the King's coach went by, calling out as loudly as he could—"Help, help! The Marquis of Carabas will be drowned."

The King looked out of the carriage window, and when he saw the Cat who had brought him so many fine rabbits and partridges, he ordered his bodyguards to fly at once to the rescue of the Marquis of Carabas.

Then the Cat came up to the carriage and told the King that while his master was bathing some robbers had stolen all his clothes. The King immediately ordered one of his own magnificent suits of clothes to be taken to the Marquis; so when the Miller's son appeared before the monarch and his daughter, he looked so handsome, and was so splendidly attired, that the Princess fell in love with him on the spot.

The King was so struck with his appearance that he insisted upon his getting into the carriage to take a drive with them. The Cat, delighted with the way his plans were turning out, ran on before. He reached a meadow where some peasants were making hay.

"Good people," said he, "if you do not tell the King, when he comes this way, that the meadow you are mowing belongs to the Marquis of Carabas, you shall all be chopped up into little pieces."

When the King came by, he stopped to ask the haymakers to whom the meadow belonged. "To the Marquis of Carabas, if it please Your Majesty," answered they, trembling, for the Cat's threat had frightened them terribly.

The Cat, who continued to run before the carriage, now came to some reapers. "Good

H·M·BROCK·

people," said he, "if you do not tell the King that all this corn belongs to the Marquis of Carabas, you shall all be chopped up into little pieces."

The King again stopped to ask to whom the land belonged, and the reapers, obedient to the Cat's command, answered— "To the Marquis of Carabas, please Your Majesty."

And all the way the Cat kept running on before the carriage, repeating the same instructions to all the laborers he came to, so that the King became very astonished at the vast possessions of the Marquis of Carabas.

At last the Cat arrived at a great castle, where an Ogre lived who was very rich, for all the lands through which the King had been riding were part of his estate. The Cat knocked at the castle door, and asked to see the Ogre.

The Ogre received him very civilly, and asked him what he wanted.

"If you please, sir," said the Cat, "I have heard that you have the power of changing yourself into any sort of animal you please— and I came to see if it could possibly be true."

"So I have," replied the Ogre, and in a moment he turned himself into a lion. This gave the Cat a great fright, and he scrambled up the curtains to the ceiling.

"Indeed, sir," he said, "I am now quite convinced of your power to turn yourself into such a huge animal as a lion, but I do not suppose you can change yourself into a small one— such as a mouse, for instance."

"Indeed, I can," cried the Ogre, indignantly, and in a moment the lion had vanished, while a little brown mouse frisked about the floor.

In less than half a second the Cat sprang down from the curtains and, pouncing upon the mouse, ate him all up before the Ogre had time to return to any other shape.

And when the King arrived at the castle gates, there stood the Cat upon the doorstep, bowing and saying— "Welcome to the castle of the Marquis of Carabas!"

The Miller's son, now the Marquis of Carabas thanks to his cat, helped the King and the Princess to alight, and the Cat led them into a great hall, where a feast had been spread for the Ogre.

H·M·BROCK

The King was so delighted with the good looks, the charming manners, and the great wealth of the Marquis of Carabas, that he said the Marquis must marry his daughter.

The Marquis, of course, replied that he should be only too happy, and the very next day he and the Princess were married.

As for the Cat, he was given the title of Puss-in-Boots, and ever after only caught mice for his own amusement.

Snow White

t was the middle of winter, when the broad flakes of snow were falling around, that the Queen of a country many thousand miles off sat working at her window. The frame of the window was made of fine black ebony, and as she sat looking out upon the snow, she pricked her finger, and three drops of blood fell upon it. Then she gazed thoughtfully upon the red drops that sprinkled the white snow, and said, "Would that my little daughter may be as white as that snow, as red as that blood, and as black as this ebony window frame!" And so the little girl really did grow up; her skin was as white as snow, her cheeks as rosy as the blood, and her hair as black as ebony— and she was called Snow White.

But this Queen died. The King soon married another wife, who became Queen, and was very beautiful, but so vain that she could not bear to think that anyone could be more beautiful than she was. She had a fairy looking-glass, to which she used to go, and then she would gaze upon herself in it, and say:

"Tell me, glass, tell me true!
Of all the ladies in the land,
Who is fairest, tell me, who?"

And the glass had always answered:

"Thou, Queen, art the fairest in all the land."

But Snow White grew more and more beautiful, and when she was seven years old she was as bright as the day, and fairer than the Queen herself. Then the glass one day answered the Queen, when she went to look in it as usual:

"Thou, Queen, art fair, and beauteous to see,
But Snow White is lovelier far than thee!"

When she heard this, the Queen turned pale with rage and envy, and called to one of her servants, and said, "Take Snow White away into the wide wood, that I may never see her

any more." Then the servant led her away; but his heart melted when Snow White begged him to spare her life, and he said, "I will not hurt you, thou pretty child." So he left her by herself, and though he thought it most likely that the wild beasts would tear her in pieces, he felt as if a great weight were taken off his heart when he had made up his mind not to kill her but to leave her to her fate, with the chance of someone finding and saving her.

Then poor Snow White wandered along through the wood in great fear, and the wild beasts roared about her, but none did her any harm. In the evening she came to a cottage among the hills, and went in to rest, for her little feet would carry her no further. Everything was spruce and neat in the cottage: on the table was spread a white cloth, and there were seven little plates, seven little loaves, and seven little glasses with wine in them, and seven knives and forks laid in order, and by the wall stood seven little beds. As she was very hungry, she picked a little piece of each loaf and drank a very little wine out of each glass, and after that she thought she would lie down and rest. So she tried all the little beds, but one was too long, and another was too short, till at last the seventh suited her, and there she laid herself down and went to sleep.

By and by in came the masters of the cottage. Now they were seven little dwarfs, that lived among the mountains, and dug and searched for gold. They lighted up their seven lamps, and saw at once that all was not right.

The first said, "Who has been sitting on my stool?"
The second, "Who has been eating off my plate?"
The third, "Who has been picking at my bread?"
The fourth, "Who has been meddling with my spoon?"
The fifth, "Who has been handling my fork?"
The sixth, "Who has been cutting with my knife?"
The seventh, "Who has been drinking my wine?"

Then the first looked round and said, "Who has been lying on my bed?" And the rest came running to him, and everyone cried out that somebody had been upon his bed. But the seventh saw Snow White, and called all his brethren to come and see her; they cried out with wonder and astonishment and brought their lamps to look at her, and said, "Good heavens! What a

lovely child she is!" And they were very glad to see her, and took care not to wake her; the seventh dwarf slept an hour with each of the other dwarfs in turn, till the night was gone.

In the morning Snow White told them all her story; they pitied her, and said if she would keep all things in order, and cook and wash and knit and spin for them, she might stay where she was, and they would take good care of her. Then they went out all day long to their work, seeking for gold and silver in the mountains, but Snow White was left at home, and they warned her, and said, "The Queen will soon find out where you are, so take care and let no one in."

But the Queen, now that she thought Snow White was dead, believed that she must be the fairest lady in the land, and she went to her glass and said:

"Tell me, glass, tell me true!
Of all the ladies in the land,
Who is fairest, tell me, who?"

And the glass answered:

"Thou, Queen, art the fairest in all this land,
But over the hills, in the greenwood shade,
Where the seven dwarfs their dwelling have made,
There Snow White is hiding her head, and she
Is lovelier far, O Queen! than thee."

Then the Queen was very much frightened, for she knew that the glass always spoke the truth, and was sure that the servant had betrayed her. She could not bear to think that anyone lived who was more beautiful than she was, so she dressed herself up as an old pedlar, and went her way over the hills, to the place where the dwarfs dwelt. Then she knocked at the door, and cried, "Fine wares to sell!" Snow White looked out the window, and said, "Good day, good woman! What have you to sell?" "Good wares, fine wares," said she, "laces and bobbins of all colors." "I will let the old lady in; she seems to be a very good sort of person," thought Snow White, as she ran down and unbolted the door. "Bless me!" said the old woman, "How badly your stays are laced! Let me lace them up with one of my nice new laces."

Snow White did not dream of any mischief, so she stood before the old woman. She set to work so nimbly, and pulled the lace so tight, that Snow White's breath was stopped, and she fell down as if she were dead. "There's an end to all thy beauty," said the spiteful Queen, and went away home.

In the evening the seven dwarfs came home, and I need not say how grieved they were to see their faithful Snow White stretched out upon the ground, as if she was quite dead. However, they lifted her up, and when they found what ailed her, they cut the lace, and in a little time she began to breathe, and very soon came to life again. Then they said, "The old woman was the Queen herself; take care another time, and let no one in when we are away."

When the Queen got home, she went straight to her glass, and spoke to it as before, but to her great grief it still said:

"Thou, Queen, art the fairest in all this land,
But over the hills, in the greenwood shade,
Where the seven dwarfs their dwelling have made,
There Snow White is hiding her head, and she
Is lovelier far, O Queen! than thee."

Then the blood ran cold in her heart with spite and malice, to see that Snow White still lived, and she dressed herself up again, but in quite another dress from the one she wore before, and took with her a poisoned comb. When she reached the dwarfs' cottage, she knocked at the door, and cried, "Fine wares to sell!" But Snow White said, "I dare not let anyone in." Then the Queen said, "Only look at my beautiful combs!" and gave her the poisoned one. It looked so pretty, that she took it up and put it into her hair to try it, but the moment it touched her head, the poison was so powerful that she fell down senseless. "There you may lie," said the Queen, and went her way. But by good luck the dwarfs came in very early that evening, and when they saw Snow White lying on the ground, they guessed what had happened, and soon found the poisoned comb. When they took it away she got well, and told them all that had passed. They warned her once more not to open the door to anyone.

Meantime the Queen went home to her glass, and shook with rage when she read the very same answer as before, and she said, "Snow White shall die, if it costs me my life." So she went by herself into her chamber, and got ready a poisoned apple; the outside looked very rosy and tempting, but whoever tasted it was sure to die. Then she dressed herself up as a peasant's wife, and travelled over the hills to the dwarfs' cottage, and knocked at the door, but Snow White put her head out of the window and said, "I dare not let anyone in, for the dwarfs have told me not to." "Do as you please," said the old woman, "but at any rate take this pretty apple. I will give it you." "No," said Snow White, "I dare not take it." "You silly girl!" answered the old woman, "what are you afraid of? Do you think it is poisoned? Come! You eat one part, and I will eat the other." Now the apple was so made up that one side was good, though the other side was poisoned. Then Snow White was much tempted to taste, for the apple looked so very nice. When she saw the old woman eat, she could wait no longer. She had scarcely put the piece into her mouth, when she fell down dead upon the ground. "This time nothing will save thee," said the Queen, and she went home to her glass, and at last it said:

"Thou, Queen, art the fairest of all the fair."

And then her wicked heart was glad, and as happy as such a heart could be.

When evening came, and the dwarfs had come home, they found Snow White lying on the ground; no breath came from her lips, and they were afraid that she was quite dead. They lifted her up, and combed her hair, and washed her face with wine and water, but all was in vain, for the little girl seemed quite dead. So they laid her down upon a bier, and all seven watched and bewailed her three whole days. Then they thought they would bury her, but her cheeks were still rosy, and her face looked just as it did while she was alive, so they said, "We will never bury her in the cold ground." They made a coffin of glass, so that they might still look at her, and wrote upon it in golden letters what her name was, and that she was a King's daughter. The coffin was set among the hills, and one of the dwarfs always sat by it and watched. The birds of the air came too, and bemoaned Snow White– first of all came an owl, and then a raven, and at last a dove, and sat by her side.

And thus Snow White lay for a long, long time, and still only looked as though she was asleep, for she was even now as white as snow, and as red as blood, and as black as ebony. At last a Prince came and called at the dwarfs' house. He saw Snow White, and read what was written in golden letters. Then he offered the dwarfs money, and prayed and

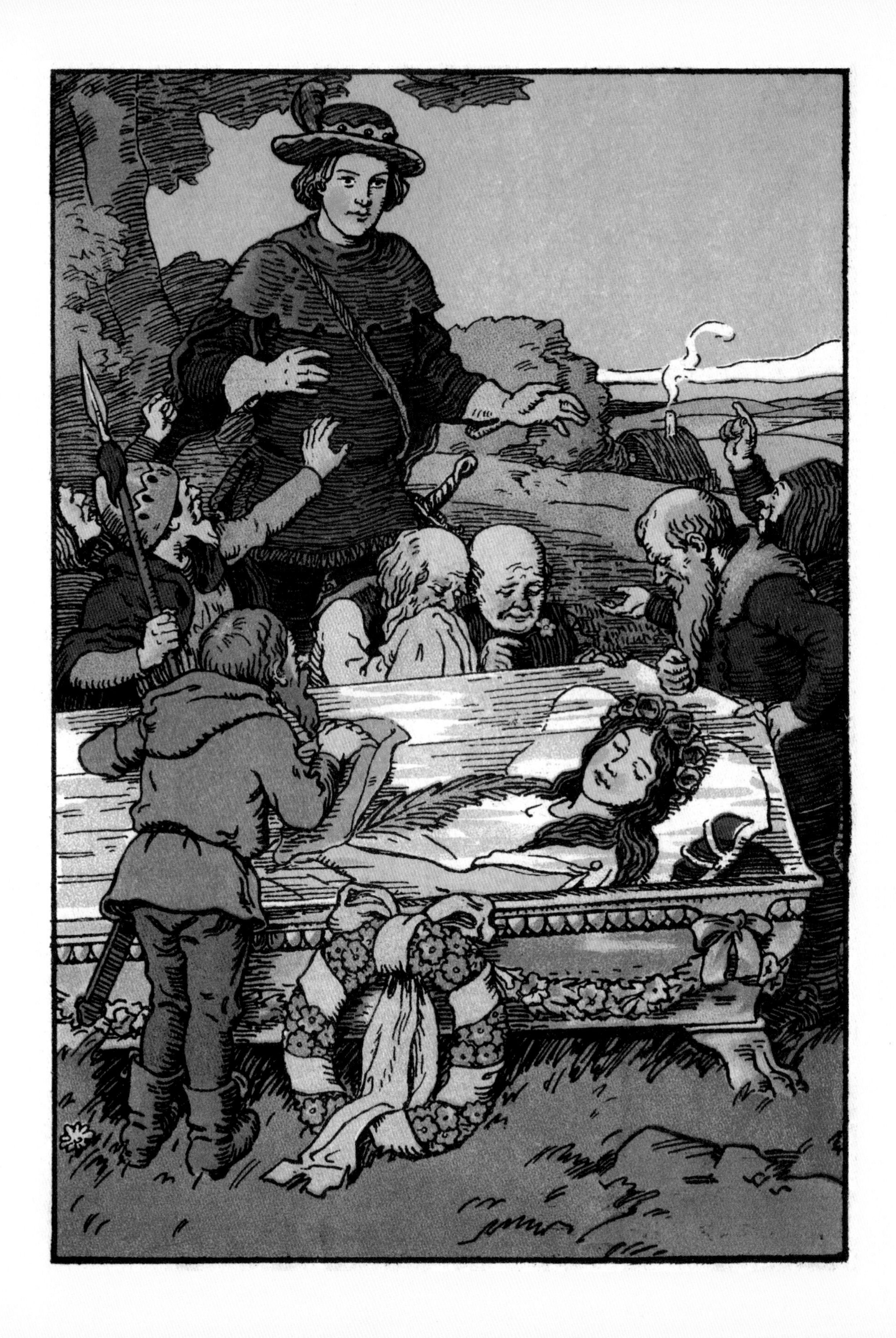

besought them to let him take her away, but they said, "We will not part with her for all the gold in the world." At last, however, they had pity on him, and gave him the coffin, but the moment he lifted it up to carry it home with him, the piece of apple fell from between her lips, and Snow White awoke, and said, "Where am I?" And the Prince said, "Thou art quite safe with me."

Then he told her all that had happened, and said, "I love you far better than all the world, so come with me to my father's palace, and you shall be my wife." And Snow White consented, and went home with the Prince, and everything was got ready with great pomp and splendor for their wedding.

To the feast was asked, among the rest, Snow White's old enemy, the Queen, and as she was dressing herself in fine rich clothes, she looked in the glass and said:

"Tell me, glass, tell me true!
Of all the ladies in the land,
Who is fairest, tell me, who?"

And the glass answered:

"Thou, lady, art loveliest here, I ween,
But lovelier far is the new-made Queen."

When she heard this, she started with rage, but her envy and curiosity were so great, that she could not help setting out to see the bride. When she got there, and saw that it was no other than Snow White, whom she thought had been dead a long while, she choked with rage, and fell down and died. But Snow White and the Prince lived and reigned happily over that land many, many years, and sometimes they went up into the mountains, and paid a visit to the little dwarfs, who had been so kind to Snow White in her time of need.

Aladdin & His Wonderful Lamp

Aladdin was a Chinese boy and lived in the great city of Peking. One day he was playing in the streets when a stranger came up to him and said: "How do you do, my boy. Don't you recognize me? I'm your uncle."

Now Aladdin had never seen the man before and didn't understand how he could be his uncle. But the stranger explained that he had always lived in Africa, and this was the first time he had been able to come to China to pay a visit to Aladdin's mother. After the stranger had given Aladdin a handful of money, the boy was quite ready to believe that he was his uncle.

"Now," said the stranger, "before I go to your house, I would like to take a walk out into the country. I hear you have beautiful mountains around here and I am very anxious to see them. Will you show me the way?"

Aladdin was willing, and together they left the city.

At last they came to some low mountains, and as they were both tired, they sat down to rest. The stranger built a fire, and as the sticks began to blaze, he threw some incense on them and said several magic words which Aladdin could not understand. Scarcely had he done so when the earth opened before them and a great stone could be seen with a brass ring fastened to it. Aladdin was so frightened that he tried to run away, but the stranger caught hold of him and held him. "Do not be afraid, my boy, but listen to what I tell you. I am a magician and have learned from my wise books that a great treasure is hidden under this rock. I am not permitted to go down after it myself, so you must go, and we will then both be richer than the greatest monarch in the world."

On hearing this, Aladdin was quite willing to do anything the magician commanded. "Take hold of the stone and lift it up," ordered the uncle. Aladdin did so, and there immediately appeared a stone staircase about three or four feet deep, leading down to a door. "Go down those steps, my boy," said the African magician, "and open the door. It will lead you into a palace of marble. Some of the rooms are very narrow, and as you pass through, you must be careful not to touch the walls, for if you do you will die instantly. When you have passed through the palace, you will come to a beautiful garden, and at the further end hangs a lighted lamp. You must take it down, blow out the flame and empty out the oil. When you have done this, bring it back to me."

After saying this, the magician took off a ring and placed it on Aladdin's finger, telling him that it was a charm and would protect him from all danger.

Aladdin descended the steps, and carefully following the directions given him, soon came to the garden and took down the lamp. He was surprised to see that the trees growing around him bore fruit made of precious stones. He gathered as many jewels as he could and hid them in his pockets and his hat. Soon he arrived back at the mouth of the cave, where the magician was awaiting him impatiently. When Aladdin saw him he cried out, "Give me your hand, Uncle, and help me up."

"Give me the lamp first," answered the man, but the lad refused to give it up, and this so angered the magician that he flew into a passion, said two magical words, and lo! the stone rolled back into place and the earth closed over as it was in the beginning.

The magician, thinking that he was leaving the boy to perish, hurried out of the city, still very angry to think that he had not been able to get the treasured lamp. His black art books had told him the secret of the lamp. But it was forbidden him to go down into the cave. It had to be given to him willingly by another person, so that was why he had asked Aladdin to go after it for him.

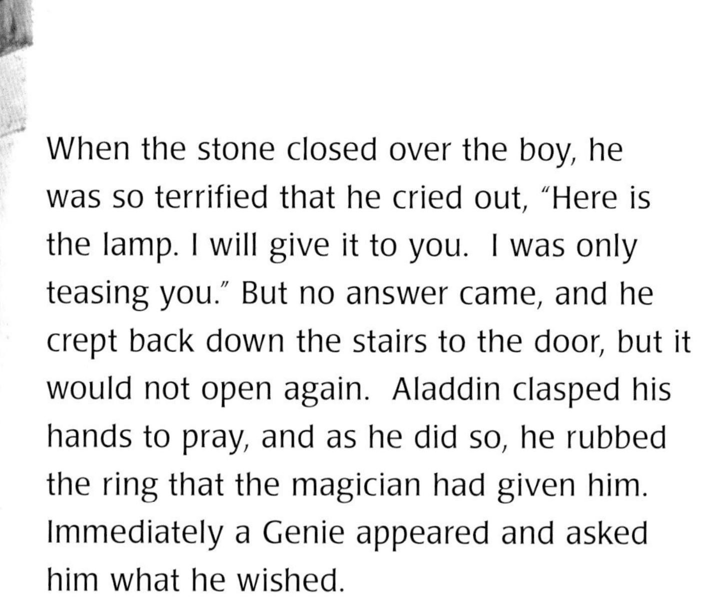

When the stone closed over the boy, he was so terrified that he cried out, "Here is the lamp. I will give it to you. I was only teasing you." But no answer came, and he crept back down the stairs to the door, but it would not open again. Aladdin clasped his hands to pray, and as he did so, he rubbed the ring that the magician had given him. Immediately a Genie appeared and asked him what he wished.

"Oh, please get me out of this dreadful place," cried Aladdin. He had no sooner spoken these words than he found himself back in his own home. He related his adventures to his mother, and she was so astonished she could hardly believe her ears. She glanced at the lamp, and as it was so dull looking, she began to shine it with her apron. No sooner had she touched it than a hideous Genie of gigantic size appeared and asked her what she desired.

She was too terrified to speak, but Aladdin snatched the lamp out of her hand and said boldly, "We are hungry; bring us something to eat." Immediately, delicious fruits and meats in solid silver dishes appeared, and they sat down and had a bountiful dinner.

When the mother's hunger was satisfied she begged Aladdin to sell the lamp, as it would surely bring harm to them in the end. "You know," she said, "that our prophet has told us many times that Genies are nothing but devils."

But Aladdin knew it was a wonderful lamp and would not part with it. He hid it away, however, where it would not bother his mother.

One day the emperor's daughter, Budder-al Buddoor was driving through the Park of the Camellias, when Aladdin happened to see her. He was so impressed with her beauty that he made up his mind then and there that he would marry her. So he hastened home, gathered together the precious stones that he had brought from the enchanted garden where he found the lamp, and sent them by his mother to the emperor.

The mother reached the palace just as the great King was returning from a promenade. She handed him the precious jewels and told him that her son wished to marry the beautiful Princess. The emperor was so astonished at seeing such magnificent diamonds, emeralds, rubies, and other dazzling stones, that he told the woman that he would consider the matter and asked her to come back in three months.

In the meantime, the emperor had his jewelers examine the stones that had been given him, and they declared that they were the biggest and most wonderful precious stones in the kingdom. So Aladdin was sent for, and when he appeared at the royal court, he was told that he could marry the Princess if he could present her with forty carved golden cups filled with the same kind of precious stones.

Aladdin went home, hunted up his lamp, and after rubbing it a second or two, out sprang the terrible Genie and asked him what he wanted.

Aladdin told him his wishes and the Genie disappeared a moment and then returned with forty servants carrying the forty golden cups encrusted with diamonds, and overflowing with pearls, rubies and emeralds.

When the emperor saw them, he immediately gave his consent to the marriage, which took place the next day. In the meantime, Aladdin rubbed his lamp again and bade the Genie build him a magnificent palace, and furnish it with golden furniture. He also demanded rich clothes for his mother and himself, a retinue of servants, and horses better than any owned by the emperor.

He and his mother then rode in great state to the emperor's castle where the wedding took place amid much rejoicing.

The African magician, however, soon learned of the marriage and how the Prince had built a palace in one night, and he began to wonder if it could be that Aladdin had escaped from the cave with the magic lamp. So he traveled again to China and sought out the beautiful palace. The minute he saw it he knew that no one but the Genie of the lamp could have built it. So he determined to get the lamp away from Aladdin.

He went to a coppersmith and bought a dozen new lamps, then went about the streets calling out, "New lamps for old ones." When he passed under the Princess' window she heard him, and as she was as fond of a good bargain as any other woman, she said to one of her slaves, "There is an old lamp in the Prince's room; go and get it and bring it to me."

When the magician saw the lamp, he could hardly conceal his joy and quickly gave the Princess a bright new one for it. He then hurried out of the city, and when he came to a lonesome spot, he rubbed the lamp and out came the Genie and asked him what he desired.

"I command you immediately to transport me and the Princess' palace, with all its people, back to Africa."

Next morning when the emperor went to call on his daughter, his amazement was unbounded when he found that the castle was nowhere to be seen.

Now all this took place when Aladdin was out hunting for tigers. When he returned, his palace was gone. To make matters worse, the emperor was very angry at him and asked him what he had done with his daughter. "If the palace is not rebuilt in forty days, and my daughter returned to me, you shall immediately be put to death."

Aladdin was very sad, for he knew he was powerless to do anything without his lamp. He wrung his hands in despair, and without knowing it, touched the magic ring on his finger. Immediately a Genie appeared and asked him what he wanted.

"Return me my palace and my wife," cried he in sudden delight.

But this Genie was not as powerful as the Genie of the lamp and all he could do was transport Aladdin to Africa where the palace was now located. There he found his wife and learned from her own lips how she had traded his old lamp for a new one, and how the next morning she had found herself in an unknown country.

"But where is the lamp now?" asked Aladdin.

"The African magician carries it carefully wrapped up in his bosom. Only this morning he came to see me and showed it to me in triumph," answered his wife.

So it was planned that the Princess should invite the magician to dinner that very evening, and put some terrible poison in his wine. The unsuspecting magician drank his wine and immediately fell dead on the floor. Aladdin, who had been hiding, rushed out and seized the lamp which was hidden in his clothes. He rubbed it with a quick stroke, and out jumped the Genie and asked him what he wished.

"Take us, as well as our palace and all the people, back to the very place it came from," ordered Aladdin.

The genie bowed his head in token of obedience, and disappeared. Instantly the palace was transported back to China, and its removal was only felt by two little shocks—one when it was lifted up and the other when it was set down again.

Next morning when the emperor looked out of his windows, there stood the Princess' palace as before. He hurried over to pay a visit and to ask Aladdin's forgiveness for having threatened him with death.

Several years later the emperor died of old age, and as he had no sons, Aladdin and the Princess became the rulers of all China and lived happily ever afterward!

The Three Bears

nce upon a time there were three Bears who lived together in a house of their own in a wood. One of them was a Little Wee Bear, and one was a Middle-sized Bear, and the other was a Great Big Bear. They had each a bowl for their porridge– a little bowl for the Little Wee Bear, and a middle-sized bowl for the Middle-sized Bear, and a great bowl for the Great Big Bear. And they had each a chair to sit in– a little chair for the Little Wee Bear, and a middle-sized chair for the Middle-sized Bear, and a great chair for the Great Big Bear. And they had each a bed to sleep in– a little bed for the Little Wee Bear, and a middle-sized bed for the Middle-sized Bear, and a great bed for the Great Big Bear.

One day, after they had made the porridge for their breakfast and poured it into their porridge-bowls, they walked out into the wood while the porridge was cooling, that they might not burn their mouths by beginning too soon, for they were polite, well-brought-up Bears. While they were away, a little girl called Goldilocks, who lived at the other side of the wood and had been sent on an errand by her mother, passed by the house, and looked in at the window. She peeped in at the keyhole, for she was not at all a well-brought-up little girl. Then, seeing nobody in the house, she lifted the latch. The door was not fastened, because the Bears were good Bears, who did nobody any harm, and never suspected that anybody would harm them. So Goldilocks opened the door and went in, and well-pleased was she when she saw the porridge on the table. If she had been a well-brought-up little girl, she would have waited till the Bears came home, and then, perhaps, they would have asked her to breakfast, for they were good Bears– a little rough or so, as the manner of Bears is, but for all that very good-natured and hospitable. But she was an impudent, rude little girl, and so she set about helping herself.

First she tasted the porridge of the Great Big Bear, and that was too hot for her. Next she tasted the porridge of the Middle-sized Bear, but that was too cold for her. And then she went to the porridge of the Little Wee Bear, and tasted it, and that was neither too hot nor too cold, but just right, and she liked it so well that she ate it all up, every bit!

THE FAMILY TREE
BEAR AND FORBEAR
MAJOR URSA D.S.O.
THE BEAR TRUTH
L.L.B.

Then Goldilocks, who was tired, for she had been catching butterflies instead of running on her errand, sat down in the chair of the Great Big Bear, but that was too hard for her. And then she sat down in the chair of the Middle-sized Bear, and that was too soft for her. But when she sat down in the chair of the Little Wee Bear, that was neither too hard nor too soft, but just right. So she seated herself in it, and there she sat till the bottom of the chair came out, and down she came, plump upon the ground; that made her very cross, for she was a bad-tempered little girl.

Now, being determined to rest, Goldilocks went upstairs into the bedchamber in which the Three Bears slept. And first she lay down upon the bed of the Great Big Bear, but that was too high at the head for her. And next she lay down upon the bed of the Middle-sized Bear, and that was too high at the foot for her. And then she lay down upon the bed of the Little Wee Bear, and that was neither too high at the head nor at the foot, but just right. So she covered herself up comfortably, and lay there till she fell fast asleep.

By this time the Three Bears thought their porridge would be cool enough for them to eat it properly, so they came home to breakfast. Now careless Goldilocks had left the spoon of the Great Big Bear standing in his porridge.

"SOMEBODY HAS BEEN EATING MY PORRIDGE!" said the Great Big Bear in his great, rough, gruff voice.

Then the Middle-sized Bear looked at her porridge and saw the spoon was standing in it too.

"SOMEBODY HAS BEEN EATING MY PORRIDGE!" said the Middle-sized Bear in her middle-sized voice.

Then the Little Wee Bear looked at his, and there was the spoon in the porridge-bowl, but the porridge was all gone!

"SOMEBODY HAS BEEN EATING MY PORRIDGE, AND HAS EATEN IT ALL UP!" said the Little Wee Bear in his little wee voice.

Upon this, the Three Bears, seeing that some one had entered their house, and eaten up the Little Wee Bear's breakfast, began to look about them. Now the careless Goldilocks had not put the hard cushion straight when she rose from the chair of the Great Big Bear.

L·L·B·

"SOMEBODY HAS BEEN SITTING IN MY CHAIR!" said the Great Big Bear in his great, rough, gruff voice.

And the careless Goldilocks had squatted down the soft cushion of the Middle-sized Bear.

"SOMEBODY HAS BEEN SITTING IN MY CHAIR!" said the Middle-sized Bear in her middle-sized voice.

"SOMEBODY HAS BEEN SITTING IN MY CHAIR, AND HAS SAT THE BOTTOM THROUGH!" said the Little Wee Bear in his little wee voice.

Then the Three Bears thought they had better make a further search in case it was a burglar, so they went upstairs into their bedchamber. Now Goldilocks had pulled the pillow of the Great Big Bear out of its place.

"SOMEBODY HAS BEEN LYING IN MY BED!" said the Great Big Bear in his great, rough, gruff voice.

And Goldilocks had pulled the bolster of the Middle-sized Bear out of its place.

"SOMEBODY HAS BEEN LYING IN MY BED!" said the Middle-sized Bear in her middle-sized voice.

But when the Little Wee Bear came to look at his bed, there was the bolster in its place!

And the pillow was in its place upon the bolster!

And upon the pillow—?

There was Goldilocks' yellow head— which was not in its place, for she had no business there.

"SOMEBODY HAS BEEN LYING IN MY BED—AND HERE SHE IS STILL!" said the Little Wee Bear in his little wee voice.

Now Goldilocks had heard in her sleep the great, rough, gruff voice of the Great Big Bear, but she was so fast asleep that it was no more to her than the roaring of wind or the rumbling of thunder. And she had heard the middle-sized voice of the Middle-sized Bear, but it was only as if she had heard some one speaking in a dream. But when she heard the little wee voice of the Little Wee Bear, it was so sharp, and so shrill, that it awakened her at once. Up she started, and when she saw the Three Bears on one side of the bed,

she tumbled herself out at the other, and ran to the window. Now the window was open, because the Bears, like good, tidy Bears, as they were, always opened their bedchamber window when they got up in the morning. So naughty, frightened little Goldilocks jumped, and whether she ran into the wood and was lost there, or found her way out of the wood and got punished for being a bad girl and playing truant, no one can say. But the Three Bears never saw anything more of her.

FRANK ADAMS

Hansel & Gretel

nce upon a time there lived a woodcutter and his wife. They had two children: a boy called Hansel and a girl whose name was Gretel. The woodcutter and his family lived in a cottage on the outskirts of a forest. The man worked hard, but he could never cut down enough trees or chop up enough to earn more than a bare living.

Then a famine hit the land, and things became worse than ever.

One night, the whole family went to bed hungry, and the bad-tempered wife spoke angrily to her husband. "There is enough food for you and me," she said. "If we eat it, the children will go hungry. If we give it to them, we shall starve." "We must let the children have it," declared the kind woodcutter. "It does not matter about us."

But his wife did not agree with him. "They will suffer less is we take them into the forest and leave them there," she decided.

The woodcutter pleaded with her, but she would not listen, and at last he had to promise to carry out her wicked plan.

Now the walls were thin, and Hansel and Gretel had been able to hear all that their parents had said. "Do not worry," said the little boy to his weeping sister. "I will make sure that we can find our way home again." He opened the door and crept outside. He filled his pockets with the pebbles which were glittering like silver on the ground in the moonlight.

The next day the children's mother wakened them. "Get up!" she cried, "We are all going to the forest to fetch wood."

On the way Hansel kept stopping and looking round. "Why do you look back, Hansel?" asked his father. "I am watching my white kitten sitting on the roof," replied Hansel. But each time he stopped, Hansel threw down one of the white pebbles.

The woodcutter built a fire to keep the children warm, and then he left them. They fell

DIES
EST
FRANK ADAMS

asleep, and when they awoke it was quite dark. Poor Gretel began to cry. "Do not worry," said Hansel. He took his sister to the path and the pebbles were gleaming so brightly in the moonlight that they led the children home.

Their father was delighted to see them, but their mother scolded them, pretending that the children had lost themselves.

When things grew no better, the wicked mother decided to try the plan again, and this time Hansel could not get out to gather any pebbles.

On the way he stopped as he had done before, telling his father that he was watching his pigeon. But he was throwing down crumbs from the tiny pieces of bread he had been given.

Once more Hansel and Gretel were left behind. When night came they looked for the breadcrumbs, but, alas, the birds had eaten them!

The children tried to find their way, but every path looked the same, and soon they were lost. A shining white bird sang such a sweet song that the two children followed it down a path they had not tried before.

At the end of the winding path, the two hungry children came upon a wonderful sight. They saw a dear little cottage which was different from any other house in the world. It had walls of gingerbread and the roof was of cakes, while all the windows were of crystal clear sugar!

Hansel and Gretel began to eat pieces of the house, when the door opened and the owner peered out. The person they saw was an ugly old woman who looked like a witch. She spoke kindly to Hansel and Gretel and beckoned them inside her lovely sweetmeat house.

She gave them a wonderful meal, and when they had finished it, she showed them two little beds made up with warm blankets and soft pillows. She was so kind that Hansel and Gretel could not believe that she would do them any harm, and so they climbed into the beds and fell asleep at once.

The old woman took the smile from her face and looked very horrible indeed as she rubbed her hands together greedily. "They will make a dainty dish," she whispered. "I will eat the boy first and then his sister."

FRANK ADAMS

Poor Hansel and Gretel had fallen into a witch's trap! They were to make her a very special meal.

Early the next morning, the old woman seized the sleeping Hansel in a bony hand and thrust him into a big cage before she wakened Gretel. "Get up, lazybones, and cook the breakfast for your brother," she shouted. "You must feed him up until he is plump and tender enough for me to eat!"

Poor Gretel had to do what she was told. She cooked so much food for her brother that he soon grew plump.

Now the old witch could not see well, and so she could not discover how fat Hansel was growing. "Put out your finger, boy," she cried. "I can tell from that whether you are ready for my dinner."

Clever Hansel poked a bone through the bars of his cage. The old woman grasped it and frowned because what she thought was his finger was far too thin. The rest of him would not make a good meal for her.

Every day the witch went to the cage and felt the bone Hansel pushed out. Then she would leave him, muttering that he was far too thin.

Poor little Gretel cooked all the lovely meals the witch insisted Hansel must eat. All the witch would let her have were the scraps, and the old hag saw to it that Gretel did not have too many of those. So as Hansel grew very plump indeed, Gretel became very thin.

The days went by, and then weeks, until a whole month had passed. Hansel sat in his cage, longing to get out and run about, but still eating all the good things poor Gretel had cooked for him. The little girl worked hard in the cottage, and she was the best servant the old woman had ever had. She cleaned the cottage until it was spick and span, mopping the floors and polishing the furniture.

She made gingerbread and cake to repair the walls and roof of the magic cottage. All the time she tried to think of a plan to help Hansel out of his cage so that they could both escape.

The old witch could not see well, but her ears were very sharp. She did not miss one word the brother and sister said to one another, and so it seemed as if they would have to stay

FRANK
ADAMS

there until they were eaten up.

At last the old woman grew tired of waiting for Hansel to grow plump enough. "He will never get fat," she cried. "I will not wait any longer for my tasty meal. Whether he is fat or thin, I shall eat him tomorrow!"

Poor Gretel cried as she cleaned up the cottage. Then she went for the water the old woman wanted, ready for the next day's big feast. When morning came, the witch made Gretel stoke up the fire so that the oven was hot enough to cook poor Hansel. "First we will bake," said the old woman. "The fire must be very hot for that. Pile on more sticks girl, while I make the dough and knead it." Gretel stoked the fire until the flames shot out hungrily, while the old witch kneaded the dough into a big, round loaf.

"You must tell me if the oven is hot enough, child," demanded the witch. The wicked old woman had decided to push Gretel into the oven and eat her before she started cooking Hansel. Gretel went to the oven. "How can I tell if the oven's hot enough?" she asked. "Creep inside," cackled the old witch. "Then you will know." Gretel pretended not to understand. "I do not know how to do it," she said. "Please show me the way."

"You are a silly goose!" cried the old witch. "The oven is quite big enough for you to climb in and see for yourself. Gretel pretended to try. "The oven is too small. I cannot get in," she declared. "The opening is quite big enough," snarled the witch. "See, I could get in myself if I wanted to." She went to the oven and poked her head inside the door, which was just what Gretel was hoping she would do. The little girl gave the old woman a push and into the oven she went, which was the end of her.

Gretel rushed across to Hansel's cage and opened the door so that he could escape. He jumped out, and he and Gretel joined hands and danced round the witch's kitchen, which looked a much better place without her. Then Gretel made a meal, which this time she was able to enjoy with her brother.

"Now we must decide what to do," said Hansel. "We must go home, of course!" cried Gretel. But Hansel remembered what had happened to them before. "Let us stay in the cottage and look round first," he said. "Perhaps the old witch has some treasures hidden away."

The brother and sister went into each room in the house. In every corner they found bags

FRANK·ADAMS

of gold and precious stones which the old woman had stolen from the unfortunate people who had crossed her path. Hansel packed his pockets with pearls, diamonds and rubies, while Gretel filled her apron. Then they picked up the bags of golden money and set off to find their way home once more.

When they finally found their way home, it looked just as it had when they had left it, but inside the house things were not the same. The wicked mother had died, and their father was sitting alone. He was mourning his unkindness to his children, as he had done every day since they had gone.

Hansel and Gretel threw themselves into their father's arms, and he hugged and kissed them. "I shall never send you away again," he cried. "Some way we will manage, however poor we are." Then Hansel, with his father looking on in amazement, emptied the precious stones out of his pockets, and Gretel spilled her apronful on to the table.

After that they gave their father the bags of gold, and there is no doubt at all that they lived together happily ever after.

Beauty & the Beast

here was once a very rich merchant who had three daughters. His daughters were extremely handsome, especially the youngest. When she was little everybody admired her, and called her "The Little Beauty;" so that, as she grew up, she still went by the name of Beauty, which made her sisters very jealous.

The youngest was indeed handsomer, but also better natured than her sisters. The two eldest had a great deal of pride, because they were rich. They gave themselves ridiculous airs, and would not visit other merchants' daughters, nor keep company with any but persons of quality. They went out every day to parties of pleasure, balls, plays, concerts, and so forth, and they laughed at their youngest sister, because she spent the greatest part of her time in reading good books.

All at once the merchant lost his whole fortune, excepting a small country house at a great distance from town, and told his children with tears in his eyes they must go there and work for their living. The two eldest answered that they would not leave the town, for they had several lovers, who they were sure would be glad to have them, though they had no fortune, but the good ladies were mistaken, for their lovers slighted and forsook them in their poverty. Everybody was very glad to see their pride humbled. But they were extremely concerned for Beauty; she was such a charming, sweet-tempered creature, spoke so kindly to poor people, and was of such an affable, obliging behavior. Nay, several gentlemen would have married her, though they knew she had not a penny, but she told them she could not think of leaving her poor father in his misfortunes, but was determined to go along with him into the country to comfort and attend him. Poor Beauty at first was sadly grieved at the loss of her fortune, "but," said she to herself, "were I to cry ever so much, that would not make things better. I must try to make myself happy without a fortune."

When they came to their country house, the merchant applied himself to husbandry and tillage; Beauty rose at four in the morning, and made haste to have the house clean, and dinner ready for the family. In the beginning she found it very difficult, for she had not been used to work as a servant, but soon she grew stronger and healthier than ever. After she had done her work, she read, played on the harpsichord, or else sung whilst she spun.

On the contrary, her two sisters did not know how to spend their time; they got up at ten, and did nothing but saunter about the whole day, lamenting the loss of their fine clothes and acquaintances. "Do but see our youngest sister," said they, one to the other, "what a poor, stupid, mean-spirited creature she is, to be contented with such an unhappy, dismal situation."

The good merchant was of quite a different opinion; he knew very well that Beauty outshone her sisters, in her person as well as her mind, and admired her industry, but above all her humility and patience. Her sisters not only left her all the work of the house to do, but insulted her every moment.

The family had lived about a year in this retirement when the merchant received a letter with an account that a vessel, on board of which he had effects, was safely arrived. This news quite turned the heads of the two eldest daughters, who immediately flattered themselves with the hopes of returning to town, for they were weary of a country life. When they saw their father ready to set out, they begged of him to buy them new gowns, headdresses, ribbons, and all manner of trifles. Beauty asked for nothing, for all the money her father was going to receive would scarce be sufficient to purchase everything her sisters wanted.

"What will you have, Beauty?" said her father.

"Since you have the goodness to think of me," answered she, "be so kind to bring me a rose, for as none grows hereabouts, they are a kind of rarity." Not that Beauty cared for a rose, but she asked for something, lest she should seem by her example to condemn her sisters' conduct, who would have said she did it only to look particular.

The good man went on his journey, but when he arrived, they went to law with him about the merchandise, and after a great deal of trouble and pains to no purpose, he came back as poor as before.

He was within thirty miles of his own house, thinking on the pleasure he should have in seeing his children again, when going through a large forest he lost himself. It rained and snowed terribly; the wind was so high that it threw him twice off his horse, and night coming on, he began to fear being either starved to death with cold and hunger, or else devoured by the wolves, whom he heard howling all round him. All of a sudden, looking through a long walk of trees, he saw a light at some distance, and, going on a little farther, perceived that it came from a place illuminated from top to bottom. The merchant returned God thanks for this happy discovery, and hastened to the place, but was greatly surprised at not meeting with anyone in the outer courts. His horse followed him, and seeing a large stable open, went in. Finding both hay and oats, the poor beast, who was almost famished, fell to eating very heartily. The merchant tied him up to the manger and walked towards the house, where he saw no one. Entering into a large hall, he found a good fire and a table plentifully set out with but one place set. As he was wet quite through with the rain and snow, he drew near the fire to dry himself. "I hope," said he, "the master of the house, or his servants, will excuse the liberty I take; I suppose it will not be long before some of them appear."

He waited a considerable time, until it struck eleven, and still nobody came. At last he was so hungry that he could stay no longer, but took a chicken and ate it in two mouthfuls, trembling all the while. After this, he drank a few glasses of wine, and, growing more courageous, he went out of the hall and crossed through several grand apartments with magnificent furniture, until he came into a chamber, which had an exceedingly good bed in it, and as he was very much fatigued, and it was past midnight, he concluded it was best to shut the door and go to bed.

It was ten the next morning before the merchant waked, and as he was going to rise, he was astonished to see a good suit of clothes in place of his own, which were quite spoiled. "Certainly," said he, "this palace belongs to some kind fairy, who has seen and pitied my distress." He looked through a window, but instead of snow, saw the most delightful arbors, interwoven with beautiful flowers. He then returned to the great hall, where he had supped the night before, and found some chocolate ready made on a little table. "Thank you, good Madam Fairy," said he aloud, "for being so careful as to provide me a breakfast; I am extremely obliged to you for all your favors."

The good man drank his chocolate and then went to look for his horse, but passing through an arbor of roses, he remembered Beauty's request to him and picked a rose. Immediately he heard a great noise, and saw such a frightful Beast coming towards him, that he was ready to faint away.

"You are very ungrateful," said the Beast to him, in a terrible voice. "I have saved your life by receiving you into my castle, and, in return, you steal my roses, which I value beyond anything in the universe. You shall die for it; I give you but a quarter of an hour to prepare yourself, and say your prayers."

The merchant fell on his knees, and lifted up both his hands. "My Lord," said he, "I beseech you to forgive me, indeed I had no intention of offending in gathering a rose for one of my daughters, who desired me to bring her one."

"My name is not My Lord," replied the monster, "but Beast; I don't love compliments, not I. I like people to speak as they think, and so do not imagine I am to be moved by any flattering speeches. But you say you have daughters. I will forgive you, on condition that one of them come willingly, and suffer for you. Let me have no words, but go about your business, and swear that if your daughter refuses to die in your stead, you will return within three months."

The merchant had no mind to sacrifice his daughters to the ugly monster, but he thought, in obtaining this respite, he should have the satisfaction of seeing them once more, so he promised, upon oath, he would return, and the Beast told him he might set out when he pleased, "but," added he, "you shall not depart empty handed; go back to the room where you lay, and you will see a great empty chest; fill it with whatever you like best, and I will send it to your home." Then the Beast withdrew.

"Well," said the good man to himself, "if I must die, I shall have the comfort, at least, of leaving something to my poor children." He returned to the bedchamber, and, finding a great quantity of broad pieces of gold, he filled the great chest the Beast had mentioned, locked it, and afterwards took his horse out of the stable, leaving the palace with as much grief as he had entered it with joy. The horse, of his own accord, took one of the roads of the forest, and in a few hours the good man was at home.

His children came round him, but instead of receiving their embraces with pleasure, he looked on them, and, holding up the branch he had in his hands, he burst into tears. "Here, Beauty," said he, "take this rose. You could not have known how dearly it will cost your unhappy father," and then related his fatal adventure. Immediately the two eldest set up lamentable outcries, and said all manner of ill-natured things to Beauty, who did not cry at all.

“Do but see the pride of that little wretch,” said they; “she would not ask for fine clothes, as we did, but Miss wanted to distinguish herself, so now she will be the death of our poor father, and yet she does not so much as shed a tear.”

“Why should I,” answered Beauty. “It would be very needless, for my father shall not suffer upon my account, since the monster will accept one of his daughters. I will deliver myself up to all his fury, and I am very happy in thinking that my death will save my father’s life, and be a proof of my tender love for him.”

“I am charmed with Beauty’s kind and generous offer, but I cannot yield to it. I am old, and have not long to live, so can only lose a few years, which I regret for your sakes alone, my dear children,” said the merchant.

“Indeed father,” said Beauty, “you shall not go to the palace without me; you cannot hinder me from following you.” It was to no purpose all they could say. Beauty still insisted on setting out for the fine palace, and her sisters were delighted at it, for her virtue and amiable qualities made them envious and jealous.

The merchant was so afflicted at the thought of losing his daughter that he had quite forgotten the chest full of gold, but at night when he retired to rest, no sooner had he shut his chamber door, than, to his great astonishment, he found it by his bedside. He was determined, however, not to tell his children that he was grown rich, because they would have wanted to return to town, and he was resolved not to leave the country. But he trusted Beauty with the secret, who informed him that two gentlemen came in his absence, and courted her sisters. She begged her father to consent to their marriage, and give them fortunes, for she was so good that she loved them and forgave heartily all their ill usage. These wicked creatures rubbed their eyes with an onion to force some tears when they parted with their sister. Beauty was the only one who did not shed tears at parting, because she would not increase their uneasiness.

The horse took the direct road to the palace, and towards evening they perceived it illuminated as at first. The horse went by himself into the stable, and the good man and his daughter came into the great hall, where they found a table splendidly served up, and two places set. The merchant had no heart to eat, but Beauty, endeavoring to appear cheerful, sat down to table and served them both. She thought to herself, “Beast surely has a mind

to fatten me before he eats me, since he provides such plentiful entertainment." When they had supped, they heard a great noise, and the merchant, all in tears, bid his poor child farewell, as he heard Beast was coming. Beauty was sadly terrified at his horrid form, but she took courage as well as she could, and when the monster asked her if she came willingly, "ye – e – es," said she, trembling.

The beast responded, "You are very good, and I am greatly obliged to you. Honest man, go your way tomorrow morning, but never think of coming here again."

"Farewell, Beast," answered the merchant, and immediately the monster withdrew. "Oh, daughter," said the merchant, embracing Beauty, "I am almost frightened to death, believe me, you had better go back, and let me stay here."

"No, Father," said Beauty, in a resolute tone, "you shall set out tomorrow morning and leave me to the care and protection of providence." They went to bed and thought they should not close their eyes all night. Scarce were they laid down, then they fell fast asleep, and Beauty dreamed that a fine lady came, and said to her, "I am content, Beauty, with your good will; this good action of yours in giving up your own life to save your father's shall not go unrewarded." Beauty waked and told her father her dream, and though it helped to comfort him a little, he could not help crying bitterly when he took leave of his dear child.

As soon as he was gone, Beauty sat down in the great hall and cried, too. But she was as strong as she was lovely, and resolved not to be miserable for the little time she had remaining to live, for she firmly believed Beast would eat her up that night. She thought she might as well walk about until then, and view this fine castle, which she could not help admiring. It was a delightful, pleasant place, and she was extremely surprised at seeing a door, over which was written, "Beauty's Apartment." She opened it hastily, and was quite dazzled with the magnificence there. What chiefly took her attention was a large library, a harpsichord, and several music books. "Well," said she to herself, "I see they will not let my time hang heavy upon my hands for want of amusement." Then she reflected, "Were I but to stay here a day, there would not have been all these preparations." This consideration inspired her with fresh courage, and opening the library, she took a book and read these words, in letters of gold:

Welcome, Beauty, banish fear,
You are queen and mistress here.
Speak your wishes, speak your will,
Swift obedience meets them still.

"Alas," said she, with a sigh, "there is nothing I desire so much as to see my poor father and know what he is doing." She had no sooner said this when, casting her eyes on an enormous looking glass, to her great amazement, she saw her own home, where her father arrived with a very dejected countenance. Her sisters went to meet him, and, notwithstanding their endeavors to appear sorrowful, the joy they felt for having got rid of their sister was visible in every feature.

At noon she found dinner ready, and, while at table, was entertained with an excellent concert of music, though without seeing anybody. But at night, as she was going to sit down to supper, she heard the noise Beast made, and could not help being sadly terrified. "Beauty," said the monster, "will you give me leave to see you sup?"

"That is as you please," answered Beauty trembling.

"No," replied the Beast, "you alone are mistress here. You need only bid me gone, if my presence is troublesome, and I will immediately withdraw. But, tell me, do not you think me very ugly?"

"That is true," said Beauty, "for I cannot tell a lie, but I believe you are very good natured."

"So I am," said the monster, "but then, besides my ugliness, I have no sense. I know very well, that I am a poor, silly, stupid creature."

"'Tis no sign of folly to think so," replied Beauty, "for never did a fool know this, or had so humble a conceit of his own understanding."

"Eat then, Beauty," said the monster, "and endeavor to amuse yourself in your palace, for everything here is yours, and I should be very uneasy if you were not happy."

"You are very obliging," answered Beauty. "I own I am pleased with your kindness, and when I consider that, your deformity scarce appears."

"Yes, yes," said the Beast, "my heart is good, but still I am a monster."

"Among mankind," says Beauty, "there are many that deserve that name more than you, and I prefer you, just as you are, to those, who, under a human form, hide a treacherous, corrupt and ungrateful heart."

"If I had sense enough," replied the Beast, "I would make a fine compliment to thank you, but I am so dull that I can only say, I am greatly obliged to you."

Beauty ate a hearty supper, and had almost conquered her dread of the monster, but she almost fainted away when he said to her, "Beauty, will you be my wife?"

It was some time before she dared answer, for she was afraid of making him angry, if she refused. At last, however, she said trembling, "No, Beast." Immediately the poor monster sighed, and hissed so frightfully that the whole palace echoed. But Beauty soon recovered her fright, for Beast having said, in a mournful voice, "Then farewell, Beauty," left the room, and only turned back, now and then, to look at her as he went out.

When Beauty was alone, she felt a great deal of compassion for poor Beast. "Alas," said she, "'tis a thousand pities that anything so good natured should be so ugly."

Beauty spent three months very contentedly in the palace. Every evening Beast paid her a visit, and talked to her during supper very rationally with plain good common sense, but never with what the world calls wit. Beauty daily discovered valuable qualities in the monster, and seeing him often had so accustomed her to his deformity, that, far from dreading the time of his visit, she would often look on her watch to see when it would be nine, for the Beast never missed coming at that hour. There was but one thing that gave Beauty any concern, which was that every night, before she went to bed, the monster always asked her if she would be his wife. One day she said to him, "Beast, you make me very uneasy, I wish I could consent to marry you, but I am too sincere to make you believe that will ever happen. I shall always esteem you as a friend; endeavor to be satisfied with this."

"I must," said the Beast, "for, alas! I know too well my own misfortune, but then I love you with the tenderest affection. However, I ought to think myself happy that you will stay here. Promise me never to leave me."

Beauty blushed at these words. She had seen in her glass, that her father had pined himself sick for the loss of her, and she longed to see him again. "I could," answered she, "indeed, promise never to leave you entirely, but I have so great a desire to see my father, that I shall fret to death if you refuse me that satisfaction."

"I had rather die myself," said the monster, "than give you the least uneasiness. I will send you to your father, you shall remain with him, and poor Beast will die with grief."

"No," said Beauty, weeping, "I love you too well to be the cause of your death. I give you my promise to return in a week. You have shown me that my sisters are married; only let me stay a week with my father, as he is alone."

"You shall be there tomorrow morning," said the Beast, "but remember your promise. You need only lay your ring on a table before you go to bed, when you have a mind to come back. Farewell, Beauty." Beast sighed, as usual, bidding her good night, and Beauty went to bed very sad at seeing him so afflicted. When she waked the next morning, she found herself at her father's. Having rung a little bell that was by her bedside, the maid came, and the moment she saw Beauty gave a loud shriek, at which the good man ran up stairs, and thought he might die of joy to see his dear daughter again. He held her fast, locked in his arms above a quarter of an hour. As soon as the first transports were over, Beauty began to think of rising, and was afraid she had no clothes to put on. But the maid told her that a large trunk full of gowns covered with gold and diamonds had appeared in the next room. Beauty thanked good Beast for his kind care, and taking one of the plainest of them, planned to make a present of the others to her sisters. She scarce had said so when the trunk disappeared. Her father told her that Beast insisted on her keeping them herself, and immediately both gowns and trunk came back again.

Beauty dressed herself, and in the meantime, they sent for her sisters who hastened thither with their husbands. They were both of them very unhappy. The eldest had married a gentleman, extremely handsome indeed, but so fond of his own person, that he was full of nothing but his own dear self, and neglected his wife. The second had married a man of wit, but he only made use of it to plague and torment everybody, and his wife most of all. Beauty's sisters sickened with envy when they saw her dressed like a Princess, and more beautiful than ever, nor could all her affectionate behavior stifle their jealousy. They were ready to burst when she told them how happy she was. They went down into the garden to vent it in tears, and asked each other in what way this little creature was better than them, that she should be so much happier? "Sister," said the eldest, "a thought just strikes my mind; let us endeavor to detain her above a week, and perhaps the silly monster will be so enraged at her for breaking her word, that he will devour her."

"Right, Sister," answered the other. "Therefore we must show her as much kindness as possible." After they had taken this resolution, they went up and behaved so affectionately to their sister that poor Beauty wept for joy. When the week was expired, they cried and tore their hair, and seemed so sorry to part with her, that she promised to stay a week longer.

In the meantime, Beauty could not help reflecting on the uneasiness she was likely to cause poor Beast, whom she sincerely loved, and really longed to see again. The tenth night she spent at her father's, she dreamed she was in the palace garden, and that she saw Beast extended on the grass. He seemed to be expiring and, in a dying voice, reproached her with her ingratitude. Beauty started out of her sleep and burst into tears. "Am I not very wicked," said she, "to act so unkindly to Beast, who has studied so much to please me in everything? Is it his fault if he is so ugly, and has so little sense? He is kind and good, and that is sufficient. Why did I refuse to marry him? I should be happier with the monster than my sisters are with their husbands. It is neither wit, nor a fine person in a husband, that makes a woman happy, but virtue, sweetness of temper and complaisance, and Beast has all these valuable qualities. It is true, I do not feel the tenderness of affection for him, but I find I have the highest gratitude, esteem, and friendship. I will not make him miserable; were I to be so ungrateful I should never forgive myself." Beauty, having said this, rose, put her ring on the table, and then laid down again; scarce was she in bed before she fell asleep, and when she waked the next morning, she was overjoyed to find herself in the Beast's palace.

She put on one of her richest suits to please him and waited for evening with the utmost impatience. At last the wished-for hour came, the clock struck nine, yet no Beast appeared. Beauty then feared she had been the cause of his death; she ran crying and wringing her hands all about the palace, like one in despair. After having sought for him everywhere, she recollected her dream, and flew to the canal in the garden, where she dreamed she had seen him. There she found poor Beast stretched out, quite senseless, and, as she imagined, dead. She threw herself upon him without any dread, and finding his heartbeat still, she fetched some water from the canal and poured it on his head. Beast opened his eyes and said to Beauty, "You forgot your promise, and I was so afflicted for having lost you, that I resolved to starve myself, but since I have the happiness of seeing you once more, I die satisfied."

"No, dear Beast," said Beauty, "you must not die. Live to be my husband. From this moment I give you my hand and swear to be none but yours. Alas! I thought I had only a friendship for you, but the grief I now feel convinces me that I cannot live without you." Beauty scarce had pronounced these words, when she saw the palace sparkle with light. Fireworks, instruments of music and everything seemed to give notice of some great event. But nothing could fix her attention. She turned to her dear Beast, for whom she trembled with fear but how great was her surprise! Beast was disappeared, and she saw at her feet one of the loveliest Princes that eyes ever beheld. This Prince returned her thanks for having put an end to the charm under which he had so long resembled a Beast. Though this Prince was worthy of all her attention, she could not forbear asking where Beast was.

"You see him at your feet," said the Prince. "A wicked fairy had condemned me to remain under that shape until a beautiful virgin should consent to marry me. The fairy likewise enjoined me to conceal my understanding. There was only you in the world generous enough to be won by the goodness of my temper, and even in offering you my crown, I can't discharge the obligations I have to you."

Beauty, agreeably surprised, gave the charming Prince her hand to rise. They went together into the castle, and Beauty was overjoyed to find, in the great hall, her father and her whole family, whom the beautiful lady that appeared to her in her dream had conveyed thither.

"Beauty," said this lady, "come and receive the reward of your judicious choice. You have preferred virtue before either wit or beauty, and deserve to find a person in whom all these qualities are united. You are going to be a great queen. I hope the throne will not lessen your virtue, or make you forget yourself. As to you, ladies," said the fairy to Beauty's two sisters, "I know your hearts, and all the malice they contain. Become two statues, but, under this transformation, still retain your reason. You shall stand before your sister's

palace gate, and be it your punishment to behold her happiness. It will not be in your power to return to your former state until you own your faults, but I am very much afraid that you will always remain statues. Pride, anger, gluttony and idleness are sometimes conquered, but the conversion of a malicious and envious mind is a kind of miracle."

Immediately the fairy gave a stroke with her wand, and in a moment all that were in the hall were transported into the Prince's dominions. His subjects received him with joy. He married Beauty and lived with her many years, and their happiness– as it was founded on virtue– was complete.

Three Little Pigs

Once three little pigs set out to seek their fortunes. The first little pig asked a man for some straw with which to build a house.

Very soon a hungry wolf came along. "Let me in," cried the wolf. "No, no," said the pig. But the wolf huffed and puffed and he blew the house down.

The second little pig met a man with a bundle of twigs. He asked the man to give him some so he could build a house.

Soon the same old wolf came along. "Let me in," cried the wolf. "No, no," said the pig. But the wolf huffed and puffed and he blew the house down.

Now the third little pig met a man with a wheelbarrow full of bricks. And the man gave him enough to build a fine, strong house.

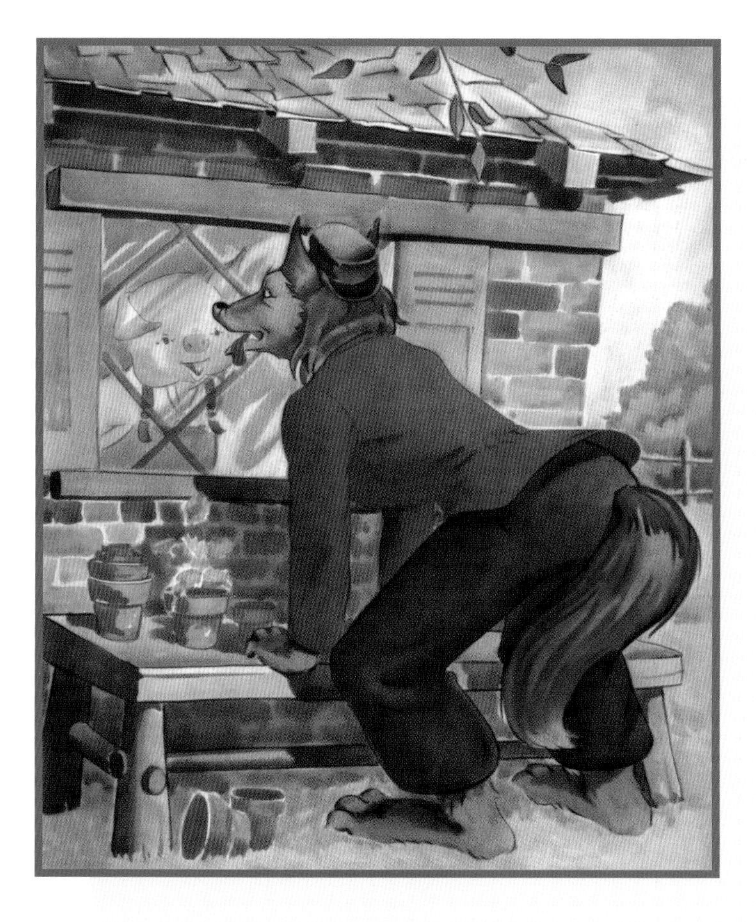

Then along came the bad wolf. "Oh, no," said the pig. The wolf huffed and puffed but he could not blow the house down. The wolf asked the pig to meet him next morning at Mr. Smith's turnip field. "All right," said the pig.

But he got up very early.

And he was back home safe and cooking his turnips by the time the wolf came around. The wolf was very angry. The wolf asked the pig to meet him next morning by a very nice apple tree. "All right," said the pig.

But he got there early and hid in the tree.

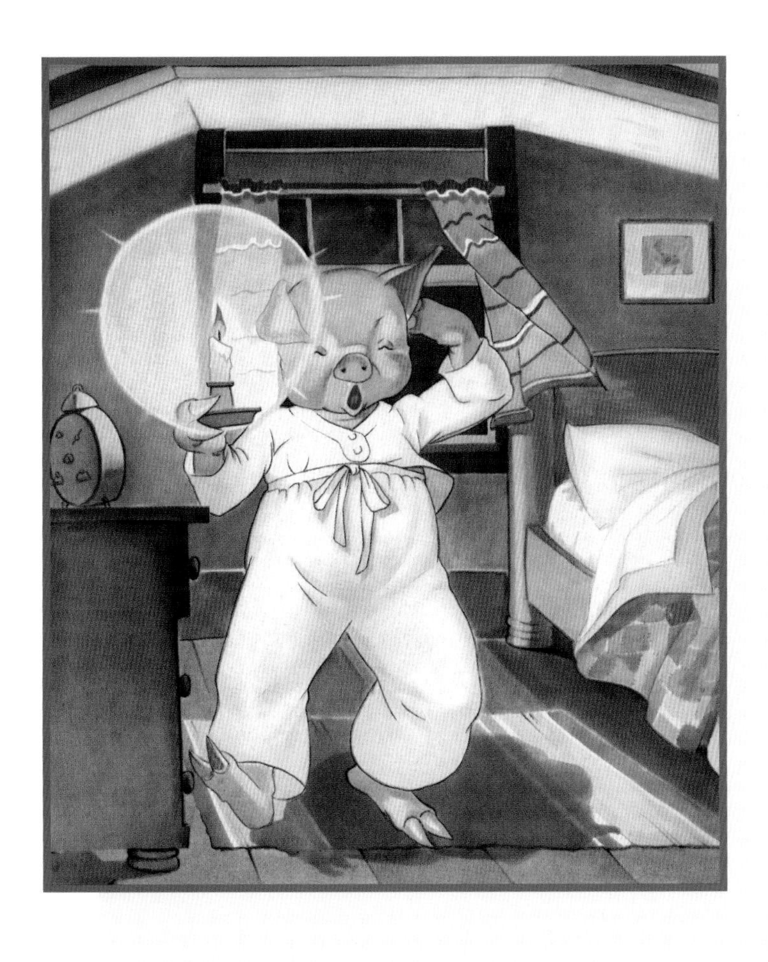

Next the wolf asked the pig to go with him to the fair. This time the pig got up while it was still as dark as night.

The pig had a very good time at the fair. He had lots of fun on the merry-go-round. When he started for home he bought a butter churn to take along.

Pretty soon along came the big, bad, hungry wolf. Into the churn the little pig leaped and he rolled past the wolf. Now the wolf was very mad. He had to catch that pig.

So he climbed up on the roof of the little pig's house and started down the chimney.

But the little pig had seen him coming. He took the lid off a large kettle of water, which was over the fire, and that ended the wolf.

Now the three little pigs all live happily together in their fine, strong house of brick.

H·M·BROCK·

Jack & the Beanstalk

There was once upon a time a poor widow who had an only son named Jack, and a cow named Milky-White. And all they had to live on was the milk the cow gave every morning, which they carried to the market and sold. But one morning Milky-White gave no milk, and they didn't know what to do. "What shall we do, what shall we do?" said the widow, wringing her hands. "Cheer up Mother, I'll go and get work somewhere," said Jack.

"We've tried that before, and nobody would take you," said his mother. "We must sell Milky-White, and with the money start a shop, or something."

"All right, Mother," says Jack. "It's market day today, and I'll soon sell Milky-White, and then we'll see what we can do."

So he took the cow's halter in his hand, and off he started. He hadn't gone far when he met a funny-looking old man, who said to him, "Good morning, Jack." "Good morning to you," said Jack, and wondered how he knew his name. "Well, Jack, and where are you off to?" said the man. "I'm going to market to sell our cow there." "Oh, you look the proper sort of chap to sell cows," said the man. "I wonder if you know how many beans make five."

"Two in each hand and one in your mouth," says Jack, as sharp as a needle.

"Right you are," says the man, "and here they are, the very beans themselves," he went on, pulling out of his pocket a number of strange-looking beans. "As you are so sharp," says he, "I don't mind doing a swap with you— your cow for these beans." "Go along," says Jack. "Wouldn't you like it?" "Ah! You don't know what these beans are," said the man. "If you plant them overnight, by morning they grow right up to the sky." "Really?" said Jack. "You don't say so." "Yes, that is so. And if it doesn't turn out to be true you can have your cow back." "Right," says Jack, and hands him over Milky-White's halter and pockets the beans.

Back goes Jack home, and as he hadn't gone very far, it wasn't dusk by the time he got to his door. "Back already, Jack?" said his mother. "I see you haven't got Milky-White, so

H·M·BROCK·

you've sold her. How much did you get for her?" "You'll never guess, Mother," says Jack. "No, you don't say so. Good boy! Five pounds? Ten? Fifteen? No, it can't be twenty." "I told you that you couldn't guess," said Jack. "What do you say to these beans? They're magical. Plant them overnight and— "

"What!" says Jack's mother. "Have you been such a fool, such a dolt, such an idiot, as to give away my Milky-White, the best milker in the parish, and prime beef to boot, for a set of paltry beans? Take that! Take that! Take that! And as for your precious beans, here they go out of the window. And now off with you to bed. Not a sup shall you drink, and not a bit shall you swallow this very night."

So Jack went upstairs to his little room in the attic, and sad and sorry he was, to be sure, as much for his mother's sake as for the loss of his supper.

At last he dropped off to sleep.

When he woke up, the room looked so funny. The sun was shining into part of it, and yet all the rest was quite dark and shady. So Jack jumped up and dressed himself and went to the window. And what do you think he saw? Why, the beans his mother had thrown out of the window into the garden had sprung up into a big beanstalk which went up and up and up till it reached the sky. So the man spoke truth after all.

The beanstalk grew up quite close past Jack's window, so all he had to do was to open it and give a jump onto the beanstalk which ran up just like a big ladder. So Jack climbed, and he climbed, and he climbed, and he climbed, and he climbed, and he climbed, and he climbed till at last he reached the sky. And when he got there, he found a long broad road going as straight as a dart. So he walked along, and he walked along, and he walked along till he came to a great big tall house, and on the doorstep there was a great big tall woman.

"Good morning, mum," says Jack, quite polite-like. "Could you be so kind as to give me some breakfast?" For he hadn't had anything to eat, you know, the night before, and was as hungry as a hunter.

"It's breakfast you want, is it?" says the great big tall woman. "It's breakfast you'll be if you don't move off from here. My man is an ogre and there's nothing he likes better than boys broiled on toast. You'd better be moving on or he'll be coming."

H·M·BROCK.

"Oh! please, mum, do give me something to eat, mum. I've had nothing to eat since yesterday morning, really and truly, mum," says Jack. "I may as well be broiled as die of hunger."

Well, the ogre's wife was not half so bad after all. So she took Jack into the kitchen, and gave him a hunk of bread and cheese and a jug of milk. But Jack hadn't half finished these when thump! thump! thump! the whole house began to tremble with the noise of someone coming.

"Goodness gracious me! It's my old man," said the ogre's wife. "What on earth shall I do? Come along quick and jump in here." And she bundled Jack into the oven just as the ogre came in.

He was a big one, to be sure. At his belt he had three calves strung up by the heels, and he unhooked them and threw them down on the table and said, "Here, wife, broil me a couple of these for breakfast. Ah! what's this I smell?

Fee-fi-fo-fum,
I smell the blood of an Englishman,
Be he alive, or be he dead,
I'll grind his bones to make my bread."

"Nonsense, dear," said his wife. "You're dreaming. Or perhaps you smell the scraps of that little boy you liked so much for yesterday's dinner. Here, you go and have a wash and tidy up, and by the time you come back your breakfast'll be ready for you."

So off the ogre went, and Jack was just going to jump out of the oven and run away when the woman told him not to. "Wait till he's asleep," says she; "he always has a doze after breakfast." Well, the ogre had his breakfast, and after that he goes to a big chest and takes out a couple of bags of gold, and down he sits and counts till at last his head begins to nod and he begins to snore till the whole house shook again.

Then Jack crept out on tiptoe from his oven, and as he was passing the ogre, he took one of the bags of gold under his arm, and off he raced till he came to the beanstalk, and then he threw down the bag of gold, which, of course, fell into his mother's garden, and then he climbed down and climbed down till at last he got home and told his mother and showed her the gold and said, "Well, Mother, wasn't I right about the beans? They are really magical, you see."

So they lived on the bag of gold for some time, but at last they came to the end of it, and Jack made up his mind to try his luck once more at the top of the beanstalk. So one fine morning he rose up early, and got onto the beanstalk, and he climbed, and he climbed, and he climbed, and he climbed, and he climbed, and he climbed till at last he came out onto the road again and up to the great tall house he had been to before. There, sure enough, was the great tall woman a-standing on the doorstep.

"Good morning, mum," says Jack, as bold as brass, "could you be so good as to give me something to eat?" "Go away, my boy," said the big tall woman, "or else my man will eat you up for breakfast. But aren't you the youngster who came here once before? Do you know, that very day my man missed one of his bags of gold." "That's strange, mum," said Jack, "I dare say I could tell you something about that, but I'm so hungry I can't speak till I've had something to eat."

Well, the big tall woman was so curious that she took him in and gave him something to eat. But he had scarcely begun munching it as slowly as he could when thump! thump! they heard the giant's footsteps, and his wife hid Jack away in the oven.

All happened as it did before. In came the ogre as he did before, said, "Fee-fi-fo-fum," and had his breakfast off three broiled oxen. Then he said, "Wife, bring me the hen that lays the golden eggs." So she brought it, and the ogre said, "Lay," and it laid an egg all of gold. And then the ogre began to nod his head, and to snore till the house shook.

Then Jack crept out of the oven on tiptoe and caught hold of the golden hen, and was off before you could say "Jack Robinson." But this time the hen gave a cackle which woke the ogre, and just as Jack got out of the house he heard him calling, "Wife, wife, what have you done with my golden hen?" And the wife said, "Why, my dear?"

But that was all Jack heard, for he rushed off to the beanstalk and climbed down like a house on fire. And when he got home he showed his mother the wonderful hen, and said "Lay" to it; and it laid a golden egg every time he said "Lay."

Well, Jack was not content, and it wasn't long before he determined to have another try at his luck up there at the top of the beanstalk. So one fine morning he rose up early and got to the beanstalk, and he climbed, and he climbed, and he climbed, and he climbed till he got to the top.

But this time he knew better than to go straight to the ogre's house. And when he got near it, he waited behind a bush till he saw the ogre's wife come out with a pail to get some water, and then he crept into the house and got into the copper. He hadn't been there long when he heard thump! thump! thump! as before, and in came the ogre and his wife.

"Fee-fi-fo-fum, I smell the blood of an Englishman," cried out the ogre. "I smell him, wife, I smell him." "Do you, my dearie?" says the ogre's wife. "Then, if it's that little rogue that stole your gold and the hen that laid the golden eggs, he's sure to have got into the oven." And they both rushed to the oven.

But Jack wasn't there, luckily, and the ogre's wife said, "There you are again with your fee-fi-fo-fum. Why, of course, it's the boy you caught last night that I've just broiled for your breakfast. How forgetful I am, and how careless you are not to know the difference between live and dead after all these years."

So the ogre sat down to the breakfast and ate it, but every now and then he would mutter, "Well, I could have sworn—" and he'd get up and search the larder and the cupboards and everything, only, luckily, he didn't think of the copper. After breakfast was over, the ogre called out, "Wife, wife, bring me my golden harp." So she brought it and put it on the table before him. Then he said, "Sing!" and the golden harp sang most beautifully. And it went on singing till the ogre fell asleep, and commenced to snore like thunder.

Then Jack lifted up the copper lid very quietly and got down like a mouse and crept on hands and knees till he came to the table, when up he crawled, caught hold of the golden harp and dashed with it towards the door. But the harp called out quite loud, "Master! Master!" and the ogre woke up just in time to see Jack running off with his harp.

Jack ran as fast as he could, and the ogre came rushing after, and would soon have caught him, only Jack had a start and dodged him a bit and knew where he was going. When he got to the beanstalk, the ogre was not more than twenty yards away when suddenly, he saw Jack disappear, and when he came to the end of the road, he saw Jack underneath climbing down for dear life. Well, the ogre didn't like trusting himself to such a

H·M·BROCK

ladder, and he stood and waited, so Jack got another start.

But just then the harp cried out, "Master! Master!" and the ogre swung himself down onto the beanstalk, which shook with his weight. Down climbs Jack, and after him climbs the ogre.

By this time Jack had climbed down and climbed down and climbed down till he was very nearly home. So he called out, "Mother! Mother! bring me an ax, bring me an ax." And his mother came rushing out with the ax in her hand, but when she came to the beanstalk she stood stock still with fright, for there she saw the ogre with his legs just through the clouds.

But Jack jumped down and got hold of the ax and gave a chop at the beanstalk, which cut it half in two. The ogre felt the beanstalk shake and quiver, so he stopped to see what was the matter. Then Jack gave another chop with the ax, and the beanstalk was cut in two and began to topple over. Then the ogre fell down and broke his crown, and the beanstalk came toppling after.

Then Jack showed his mother his golden harp, and what with showing that and selling the golden eggs, Jack and his mother became very rich, and he married a great Princess, and they lived happy ever after.

Cinderella

here was once an honest gentleman who took for his second wife a lady, the proudest and most disagreeable in the whole country. She had two daughters exactly like herself in all things. He also had one little girl, who resembled her dead mother, the best woman in all the world. Scarcely had the second marriage taken place, than the stepmother became jealous of the good qualities of the little girl, who was so great a contrast to her own two daughters. She gave her all the menial occupations of the house; compelled her to wash the floors and staircases, to dust the bed-rooms, and clean the grates. While her stepsisters occupied carpeted chambers hung with mirrors, where they could see themselves from head to foot, this poor little damsel was sent to sleep in an attic, on an old straw mattress, with only one chair and not a looking-glass in the room.

She suffered all in silence, not daring to complain to her father, who was entirely ruled by his new wife. When her daily work was done she used to sit down in the chimney-corner among the ashes, from which the two sisters gave her the nick-name of Cinderella. But Cinderella, however shabbily clad, was more beautiful than her stepsisters with all their fine clothes.

It happened that the King's son gave a series of balls, to which were invited all the rank and fashion of the city, and among the rest, the two elder sisters. They were very proud and happy, and occupied their whole time in deciding what they should wear, a source of new trouble to Cinderella, whose duty it was to get up their fine linen and laces, and who never could please them however much she tried. They talked of nothing but their clothes.

"I," said the elder, "shall wear my velvet gown and my trimmings of English lace."

"And I," added the younger, "will have my ordinary silk petticoat, but I shall adorn it with an upper skirt of flowered brocade, and shall put on my diamond tiara, which is a great deal finer than anything of yours."

Here the elder sister grew angry, and the dispute began to run so high, that Cinderella,

who was known to have excellent taste, was called upon to decide between them. She gave them the best advice she could, and gently and submissively offered to dress them herself, and especially to arrange their hair, an accomplishment in which she excelled many a noted coiffeur. The important evening came, and she exercised all her skill to adorn the two young ladies. While she was combing out the elder's hair, this ill-natured girl said sharply, "Cinderella, do you not wish you were going to the ball?"

"Ah, madam" (they obliged her always to say madam), "you are only mocking me; it is not my fortune to have any such pleasure."

"You are right; people would only laugh to see a little cinder-wench at a ball."

Any other than Cinderella would have dressed the hair all awry, but she was good, and dressed it perfectly even and smooth, and as prettily as she could.

The sisters had scarcely eaten for two days, and had broken a dozen stay-laces a day, in trying to make themselves slender, but tonight they broke a dozen more, and lost their tempers over and over again before they had finished dressing. When at last the happy moment arrived, Cinderella followed them to the coach, and after it had whirled them away, she sat down by the kitchen fire and cried.

Immediately her godmother, who was a fairy, appeared beside her. "What are you crying for, my little maid?" "Oh, I wish—I wish—" Her sobs stopped her. "You wish to go to the ball; isn't it so?" Cinderella nodded. "Well, then, be a good girl, and you shall go. First run into the garden and fetch me the largest pumpkin you can find."

Cinderella did not comprehend what this had to do with her going to the ball, but being obedient and obliging, she went. Her godmother took the pumpkin, and having scooped out all its inside, struck it with her wand; it became a splendid gilt coach, lined with rose-colored satin. "Now fetch me the mouse-trap out of the pantry, my dear."

Cinderella brought it; it contained six of the fattest, sleekest mice. The fairy lifted up the wire door, and as each mouse ran out she struck it and changed it into a beautiful black horse. "But what shall I do for your coachman, Cinderella?"

Cinderella suggested that she had seen a large black rat in the rat-trap, and he might do

for want of better. "You are right; go and look again for him."

He was found, and the fairy made him into a most respectable coachman, with the finest whiskers imaginable. She afterwards took six lizards from behind the pumpkin frame, and changed them into six footmen, all in splendid livery, who immediately jumped up behind the carriage, as if they had been footmen all their days. "Well, Cinderella, now you can go to the ball."

"What, in these clothes?" said Cinderella piteously, looking down on her ragged frock.

Her godmother laughed, and touched her also with the wand; at which her wretched thread-bare jacket became stiff with gold, and sparkling with jewels; her woolen petticoat lengthened into a gown of sweeping satin, from underneath which peeped out her little feet, no longer bare, but covered with silk stockings and the prettiest glass slippers in the world. "Now Cinderella, depart, but remember, if you stay one instant after midnight, your carriage will become a pumpkin, your coachman a rat, your horses mice, and your footmen lizards, while you yourself will be the little cinder-wench you were an hour ago."

Cinderella promised without fear, her heart was so full of joy.

When she arrived at the palace, the King's son, whom someone, probably the fairy, had told to await the coming of an uninvited Princess whom nobody knew, was standing at the entrance, ready to receive her. He offered her his hand and led her with the utmost courtesy through the assembled guests, who stood aside to let her pass, whispering to one another, "Oh, how beautiful she is!" It might have turned the head of any one but poor Cinderella, who was so used to being despised, that she took it all as if it were something happening in a dream.

Her triumph was complete; even the old King said to the Queen, that never since her majesty's young days had he seen so charming and elegant a person. All the court ladies scanned her eagerly, clothes and all, determining to have theirs made next day of exactly the same pattern. The King's son himself led her out to dance, and she danced so gracefully that he admired her more and more. Indeed, at supper, which was fortunately early, his admiration quite took away his appetite. Cinderella herself, with an involuntary shyness, sought out her sisters; she placed herself beside them and offered them all sorts of

civil attentions, which, coming as they supposed from a stranger, and so magnificent a lady, almost overwhelmed them with delight.

While she was talking with them, she heard the clock strike a quarter to twelve, and making a courteous adieu to the royal family, she re-entered her carriage, escorted tenderly by the King's son, and arrived in safety at her own door. There she found her godmother, who smiled approval, and of whom she begged permission to go to a second ball, the following night, to which the Queen had earnestly invited her.

While she was talking, the two sisters were heard knocking at the gate, and the fairy godmother vanished, leaving Cinderella sitting in the chimney-corner, rubbing her eyes and pretending to be very sleepy.

"Ah," cried the eldest sister maliciously, "it has been the most delightful ball, and there was present the most beautiful Princess I ever saw, who was so exceedingly polite to us both." "Was she?" said Cinderella indifferently, "and who might she be?" "Nobody knows, though everybody would give their eyes to know, especially the King's son."

"Indeed!" replied Cinderella, a little more interested; "I should like to see her, Miss Javotte"— that was the elder sister's name— "will you not let me go tomorrow, and lend me your yellow gown that you wear on Sundays?"

"What, lend my yellow gown to a step-wench! I am not so mad as that." At which refusal Cinderella did not complain, for if her sister really had lent her the gown she would have been considerably embarrassed.

The next night came, and the two young ladies, richly dressed in different ensembles, went to the ball. Cinderella, more splendidly attired and beautiful than ever, followed them shortly after. "Now remember twelve o'clock," was her godmother's parting speech, and she thought she certainly should. But the Prince's attentions to her were greater even than the first evening, and in the delight of listening to his pleasant conversation, time slipped by unperceived. While she was sitting beside him in a lovely alcove, and looking at the moon from under a bower of orange blossoms, she heard a clock strike the first stroke of twelve. She started up, and fled away as lightly as a deer.

Amazed, the Prince followed, but could not catch her. Indeed he missed his lovely Princess

altogether, and only saw running out of the palace doors a little dirty lass whom he had never beheld before, and of whom he certainly would never have taken the least notice. Cinderella arrived at home breathless and weary, ragged and cold, without carriage, or footmen, or coachman. The only remnant of her past magnificence was one of her little glass slippers— the other she had dropped in the ball-room as she ran away.

When the two sisters returned they were full of this strange adventure— How the beautiful lady had appeared at the ball more beautiful than ever, and enchanted every one who looked at her, and how, as the clock was striking twelve, she had suddenly risen up and fled through the ball-room, disappearing no one knew how or where, and dropping one of her glass slippers behind her in her flight. How the King's son had remained inconsolable until he chanced to pick up the little glass slipper, which he carried away in his pocket, and was seen to take it out continually, and look at it affectionately, with the air of a man very much in love. In fact, from his behavior during the remainder of the evening, all the court and royal family were convinced that he had become desperately enamored of the wearer of the little glass slipper.

Cinderella listened in silence, turning her face to the kitchen fire, and perhaps it was that which made her look so rosy, but nobody ever noticed or admired her at home, so it did not signify, and next morning she went to her weary work again just as before.

A few days after, the whole city was attracted by the sight of a herald going round with a little glass slipper in his hand, publishing, with a flourish of trumpets, that the King's son ordered this to be fitted on the foot of every lady in the kingdom, and that he wished to marry the lady whom it fitted best, or to whom it and the fellow slipper belonged. Princesses, duchesses, countesses, and simple gentlewomen all tried it on, but being a fairy slipper, it fitted nobody and beside, nobody could produce its fellow slipper, which lay all the time safely in the pocket of Cinderella's old linsey gown.

At last the herald came to the house of the two sisters, and though they well knew neither of themselves was the beautiful lady, they made every attempt to get their clumsy feet into the glass slipper, but in vain.

"Let me try it on," said Cinderella from the chimney corner.

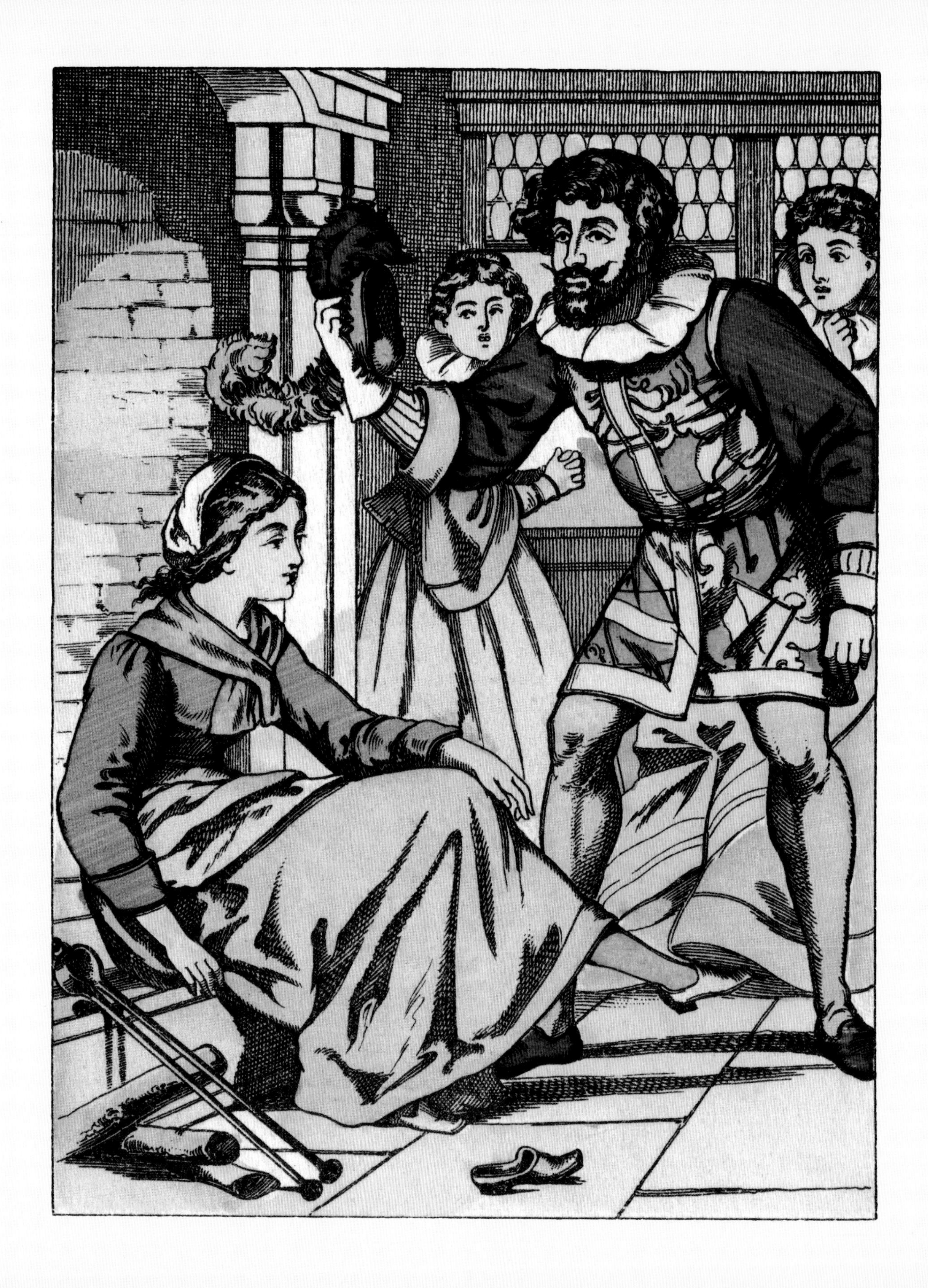

"What, you?" cried the others, bursting into shouts of laughter, but Cinderella only smiled, and held out her hand.

Her sisters could not prevent her, since the command was that every young maiden in the city should try on the slipper, in order that no chance might be left untried, for the Prince was nearly breaking his heart, and his father and mother were afraid that though a Prince, he would actually die for love of the beautiful unknown lady.

So the herald bade Cinderella sit down on a three-legged stool in the kitchen, and him-self put the slipper on her pretty little foot, which it fitted exactly; she then drew from her pocket the fellow slipper, which she also put on, and stood up— for with the touch of the magic shoes all her dress was changed likewise— no longer the poor despised cinder-wench, but the beautiful lady whom the King's son loved.

Her sisters recognized her at once. Filled with astonishment, mingled with no little alarm, they threw themselves at her feet, begging her pardon for all their former unkindness. She raised and embraced them, told them she forgave them with all her heart, and only hoped they would love her always. Then she departed with the herald to the King's palace, and told her whole story to his majesty and the royal family, who were not in the least surprised, for everybody believed in fairies, and everybody longed to have a fairy godmother.

As for the young Prince, he found her more lovely and loveable than ever, and insisted upon marrying her immediately. Cinderella never went home again, but she sent for her two sisters to the palace, and, with the consent of all parties, married them shortly after to two rich gentlemen of the court.

HASSALL

Little Red Riding Hood

Once upon a time, in a cottage near a wood, there lived a little girl. She was pretty, and good too, except when she forgot to do as she was told. Her mother loved her very much, and so did her grandmother, who lived in a cottage on the other side of the wood. This old woman made a beautiful red hood for her grandchild, which suited her so well that everybody called her Little Red Riding-Hood.

One day Red Riding-Hood's mother said to her: "My dear, I have heard that your grandmother has been ill, so I want you to go and see if she is better, and to take her these eggs, and this cream, and pat of butter. Go straight along the road to Granny's cottage, give her the nice things, and come straight home again, and tell me how she is. Do not play or idle, and do not talk to anyone by the way."

Little Red Riding-Hood was very pleased to go to see her grandmother. She put on her hood, took the basket on her arm, and started off at once. But instead of going by the road, as her mother had told her, she went through the wood because she thought it by far the prettier way. And in the wood she met an old gray wolf. Now this wolf wanted to eat her, but he was afraid to do so because some woodcutters were working not far off.

But he stopped her and said: "What have you in your basket, my dear?" Then Little Red Riding-Hood, who forgot that her mother had said she must talk to no one by the way, replied: "Some cream, and eggs, and a little pat of butter." "And where are you going, my dear?" asked the wolf. "I'm going to see Granny." "Where does Granny live, my dear?" "In the cottage beyond the wood," said the little girl. "And what do you do when you get there my dear?" "I knock at the door." "And what does your granny do then, my dear?" "She says, 'Who is there?'" "And what do you do next, my dear?" I say, 'I am Little Red Riding-Hood, and I have brought you some cream, and eggs, and a little pat of butter." "And what does Granny do next, my dear?" "She cries out 'Pull the bobbin, and the latch will go up'." When the wolf heard this, he ran off as fast as he could to the grandmother's cottage, going by the shortest way.

But Little Red Riding-Hood took the longest way, and instead of going straight along, as her mother had told her, she idled and played. She ran to and fro, picking flowers here, and gathering nuts there, making posies and chasing butterflies.

The wolf was not long in reaching Granny's cottage. He went at once to the door and knocked at it gently. "Who is there?" said a voice from within.

"I am Little Red Riding-Hood," said the wolf in a squeaky voice which he tried to make as much like a little girl's as he could "And I have brought you some cream, and eggs, and a little pat of butter." Then the grandmother, who was ill and in bed, called out: "Pull the bobbin, and the latch will go up." The wolf pulled the bobbin, and the latch went up, and the door opened. Then he ran into the cottage and sprang at once upon the old woman and gobbled her up, for he had eaten nothing for a long time and was very hungry.

Then he shut the door and put on Granny's nightgown, and nightcap, and spectacles, and got into bed to wait for Little Red Riding-Hood.

He had not long to wait. In a little while she came to the door and knocked— tap, tap. "Who is there?" asked the wolf, making his voice as soft as he could. "I am Little Red Riding-Hood, and I have brought you some cream, and eggs, and a little pat of butter," said the child. "Pull the bobbin and the latch will go up," cried the wolf.

Little Red Riding-Hood pulled the bobbin, and the latch went up, and the door opened, and she came into the cottage. The wolf drew the bed-clothes up round his head so that she could not see him very well, and said: "Shut the door, and sit down beside me, my dear."

So Little Red Riding-Hood shut the door and sat down close to the bed, and when she saw how strange her grandmother looked, she was very much astonished, and said: "Oh, Grandmamma, what great arms you have got!" "All the better to hug you, my dear," replied the wolf.

Little Red Riding-Hood was quiet for a while, and then said: "Oh, Grandmamma, what great ears you have got!" "All the better to hear you, my dear," replied the wolf.

"Oh, Grandmamma, what great eyes you have got!" said Little Red Riding-Hood after another pause. "All the better to see you, my dear," replied the wolf. Little Red Riding-Hood looked again and said: "Oh, Grandmamma, what great teeth you have got!" "All the better to eat you, my dear."

And as he said this, the wicked wolf sprang up in bed to seize the little girl and gobble her up. But at that moment the door of the cottage opened, and a woodcutter ran in. He was Red Riding-Hood's father, and he had seen his little girl go to her grandmother's cottage, and had come to fetch her home.

He soon chopped off the wicked wolf's head with his axe, and then he lifted poor Little Red Riding-Hood in his arms. She was very much frightened, and she threw her arms round his neck and cried bitterly. Then her father, holding her very tightly to make her feel quite safe, carried her home. And as he went, he sang to her these wise words:

"A little maid
Must be afraid
To do other than her mother told her;
        Of idling must be wary,
        Of gossiping be chary,
She'll learn prudence by the time that she is older."

The Ugly Duckling

t was summer. The country was lovely just then. The cornfields were waving yellow, the wheat was golden, the oats were still green, and the hay was stacked in the meadows. Beyond the fields great forests and ponds of water might be seen.

In the sunniest spot of all stood an old farmhouse with deep canals around it. At the water's edge grew great burdocks. It was just as wild there as in the deepest wood, and in this snug place sat a duck upon her nest. She was waiting for her brood to hatch.

At last one eggshell after another began to crack. From each little egg came "Cheep! cheep!" and then a little duckling's head.

"Quack! quack!" said the duck, and all the babies quacked too. Then they looked all around. The mother let them look as much as they liked, for green is good for the eyes.

"How big the world is!" said all the little ducklings.

"Do you think this is all the world?" asked the mother. "It stretches a long way on the other side of the garden and on to the parson's field, but I have never been so far as that. I hope you are all out. No, not all; that large egg is still unbroken. I am really tired of sitting so long." Then the duck sat down again.

"Well, how goes it?" asked an old duck who had come to pay her a visit.

"There is one large egg that is taking a long time to hatch," replied the mother. "But you must look at the ducklings. They are the finest I have ever seen; they are all just like their father."

"Let me look at the egg which will not hatch," said the old duck. "You may be sure that it is a turkey's egg. I was once cheated in that way. Oh, you will have a great deal of trouble, for a turkey will not go into the water. Yes, that's a turkey's egg. Leave it alone and teach the other children to swim."

"No, I will sit on it a little longer," said the mother duck.

"Just as you please," said the old duck, and she went away.

At last the large egg cracked. "Cheep! cheep!" said the young one, and tumbled out. How large it was! How ugly it was!

"I wonder if it can be a turkey chick," said the mother. "Well, we shall see when we go to the pond. It must go into the water, even if I have to push it in myself."

Next day the mother duck and all her little ones went down to the water. Splash! she jumped in, and all the ducklings went in, too. They swam about very easily, and the ugly duckling swam with them.

"No, it is not a turkey," said the mother duck. "See how well he can use his legs. He is my own child! And he is not so very ugly either."

Then she took her family into the duck yard. As they went along, she told the ducklings how to act.

"Keep close to me, so that no one can step on you," she said. "Come, now, don't turn your toes in. A well-brought-up duck turns its toes out, just like father and mother. Bow your heads before that old duck yonder. She is the grandest duck here. One can tell that by the

red rag around her leg. That's a great honor, the greatest honor a duck can have. It shows that the mistress doesn't want to lose her. Now bend your necks and say 'Quack!'"

They did so, but the other ducks did not seem glad to see them.

"Look!" they cried. "Here comes another brood, as if there were not enough of us already. And oh, dear, how ugly that large one is! We won't stand him."

Then one of the ducks flew at the ugly duckling and bit him in the neck.

"Let him alone," said the mother; "he is doing no harm."

"Perhaps not," said the duck who had bitten the poor duckling, "but he is too ugly to stay here. He must be driven out."

"Those are pretty children that the mother has," said the old duck with the rag around her leg. "They are all pretty but that one. What a pity!"

"Yes," replied the mother duck, "he is not handsome, but he is good-tempered, and he swims as well as any of the others. I think he will grow to be pretty. Perhaps he stayed too long in the egg."

"Well, make yourselves at home," said the old duck. "If you find an eel's head, you may bring it to me."

And they did make themselves at home— all but the poor ugly duckling. His life was made quite miserable. The ducks bit him, and the hens pecked him. So it went on the first day, and each day it grew worse.

The poor duckling was very unhappy. At last he could stand it no longer, and he ran away. As he flew over the fence, he frightened the little birds on the bushes.

"That is because I am so ugly," thought the duckling.

He flew on until he came to a moor where some wild ducks lived. They laughed at him and swam away from him.

Some wild geese came by, and they laughed at the duckling, too. Just then some guns went bang! bang! The hunters were all around. The hunting dogs came splash! into the swamp, and one dashed close to the duckling. The dog looked at him and went on.

"Well, I can be thankful for that," sighed he. "I am so ugly that even the dog will not bite me."

When all was quiet, the duckling started out again. A storm was raging, and he found shelter in a poor hut. Here lived an old woman with her cat and her hen. The old woman could not see well, and she thought he was a fat duck. She kept him three weeks, hoping that she would get some duck eggs, but the duckling did not lay.

After a while the fresh air and sunshine streamed in at the open door, and the duckling longed to be out on the water. The cat and the hen laughed when he told them of his wish.

"You must be crazy," said the hen. "I do

not wish to swim. The cat does not, and I am sure our mistress does not."

"You do not understand me," said the duckling. "I will go out into the wide world."

"Yes, do go," said the hen.

And the duckling went away. He swam on the water and dived, but still all the animals passed him by because he was so ugly, and the poor duckling was lonesome.

Now the winter came, and soon it was very cold. Snow and sleet fell, and the ugly duckling had a very unhappy time.

One evening a whole flock of handsome white birds rose out of the bushes. They were swans. They gave a strange cry, and spreading their great wings, flew away to warmer lands and open lakes.

The ugly duckling felt quite strange, and he gave such a loud cry that he frightened himself. He could not forget those beautiful, happy birds. He knew not where they had gone, but he wished he could have gone with them.

The winter grew cold— very cold. The duckling swam about in the water to keep from freezing, but every night the hole in which he swam became smaller and smaller. At last he was frozen fast in the ice.

Early the next morning a farmer found the duckling and took him to the farmhouse. There in a warm room, the duckling came to himself again. The children wished to play with him, but he was afraid of them.

In his terror he fluttered into the milk pan and splashed the milk about the room. The

woman clapped her hands at him, and that frightened him still more. He flew into the butter tub and then into the meal barrel.

How he did look then! The children laughed and screamed. The woman chased him with the fire tongs. The door stood open, and the duckling slipped out into the snow.

It was a cruel, hard winter, and he nearly froze. At last the warm sun began to shine, and the larks to sing. The duckling flapped his wings and found that they were strong. Away he flew over the meadows and fields.

Soon he found himself in a beautiful garden where the apple trees were in full bloom, and the long branches of the willow trees hung over the shores of the lake. Just in front of him he saw three beautiful white swans swimming lightly over the water.

"I will fly to those beautiful birds," he said. "They will kill me because I am so ugly, but it is all the same. It is better to be killed by them than to be bitten by the ducks and pecked by the hens."

So he flew into the water and swam towards the beautiful birds. They saw the duckling and came sailing down toward him. He bowed his head saying, "Kill me, oh, kill me."

But what was this he saw in the clear water? It was his own image, and lo! he was no longer a clumsy dark-gray bird, but a— swan, a beautiful white swan. It matters not if one was born in a duck yard,

if one has only lain in a swan's egg. The other swans swam around him to welcome him.

Some little children came into the garden with corn and other grains which they threw into the water. The smallest one cried, "Oh, see! There is a new swan, and it is more beautiful than any of the others."

The ugly duckling was shy and at first hid his head under his wing. Then he felt so happy that he raised his neck and said, "I never dreamed of so much happiness when I was an ugly duckling."

BRIAR · ROSE

The Sleeping Beauty

here once lived a good King and Queen who, because they had no children, were more sorry than words can tell. The great halls of the palace were silent, for there were no baby feet to patter about them, and no baby laughter to make them ring with joy. At last, however, this good Queen had a little daughter, and then a great christening was arranged. The baby Princess had for godmothers all the fairies that could be found in the land (there were seven of them), so that, when they gave their christening gifts, as fairies used to do in those days, she might have all the graces and perfections imaginable. After the christening was over, the whole company returned to the King's palace, where an elegant feast had been prepared. For each of the seven fairies a place was laid with plates of gold edged with diamonds and rubies.

But as the feasters sat down at table, there entered the banqueting-hall an old fairy who had not been invited; she had not left her tower for more than fifty years, and everyone believed that she was either dead or enchanted.

A Rackham

The King ordered a place laid for this unexpected guest, but it was impossible to give her plates of gold with diamonds and rubies, because they had made only seven for the seven fairies. The aged fairy-witch was not pleased, for she felt that she was being slighted. She muttered some threats between her teeth, and one of the young fairies sitting next to her heard them. Guessing that the witch would bestow some horrid gift upon the baby Princess, this young fairy slipped away as soon as they rose from the table, and hid behind the curtains. This she did so that she might be the last one to speak, and might undo, as far as she could, the mischief which the old witch would surely do.

The time came for the fairies to name the good things they would bestow upon the little Princess. The first said that she should be the loveliest creature in the whole world; the next, that she should be wonderfully clever; the third, that she should show matchless grace in all she did; the fourth, that she should dance perfectly; the fifth, that she should sing like a nightingale; and the sixth, that she should play charmingly upon all sorts of instruments.

The turn of the old fairy-witch had come. With shaking head, trembling even more from spite than from old age, she said that the Princess should prick her hand with a spindle, and die of the wound.

This terrible announcement made the whole company shudder, and there was not of them but wept.

At that moment the young fairy slipped from behind the curtains. "Be comforted, O King and Queen," said she. "Your daughter shall not die. It is true that I have no power to undo entirely what the old witch has done. Unhappily, the Princess will prick her hand with a spindle. But she shall not die; she shall only fall into a deep sleep that will last a hundred years. At the end of that period a King's son will come and wake her."

The King was determined to save his daughter from such a fate. He sent an order throughout all his realm, forbidding his subjects to use a spindle in spinning, or even to possess such a thing, on pain of death.

Sixteen years passed happily. Then one day, when the King and Queen were absent at one of their country houses, it happened that the Princess, wandering about the palace, went from room to room until she came at last to a little attic at the top of a tower, where an old woman sat spinning all alone. This good woman had never heard that the King had forbidden the use of a spindle.

"What are you doing my good woman?" said the Princess. "I am spinning my dear," replied the old woman, not knowing who she was. "How nice!" said the Princess. "How do you do it? Let me try; I should like to see if I can do it, too."

She took the spindle, but being very quick, and a trifle careless— and besides, what the fairies say is bound to come true!— she pricked her finger with it, and fell into a faint.

The old woman was greatly distressed. She screamed for help, and people came running from all sides. One sprinkled water on the Princess' face, one loosened her clothes, another slapped her hands, but all was of no use— she remained in her swoon.

Then the King, who had returned in haste upon hearing the news, remembered the prediction of the fairies. Knowing that what the fairies had foretold was bound to happen, he had the Princess carried to the finest room in the palace, and laid on a bed embroidered with gold and silver. She was so lovely, you would have thought her an angel; she had not lost her fresh, blooming color; her cheeks were rosy, and her lips like coral. Her eyes were closed, but they could hear her breathing gently, so they knew that she was not dead. The King gave orders that she should be left to sleep in peace until the hour of her awakening should come.

The good fairy who had saved her life was in a kingdom a dozen leagues away when the sleep came to the Princess, but she heard of it in two moments from a steward who was the happy owner of seven-league boots— quite remarkable boots in which one could cover seven leagues at a single stride. The fairy started at once, and within an hour she drove up to the palace in a chariot of fire drawn by dragons. The King himself helped her from her carriage. She told him that she approved of everything that he had done, but she felt sure that if the Princess woke a hundred years later and found herself alone in an old castle, which perhaps by that time would be in ruins, she would be frightened and unhappy. So this is what the fairy did: She touched with her wand every person in the castle, except the King and Queen—governesses, maids of honor, waiting-maids, gentlemen, officers, butlers, cooks, guards, porters, pages, and footmen. She touched also the horses in the stables, the grooms, the big watchdog in the courtyard, and even the little dog that always slept in the Princess's bed.

And as soon as she touched them, they all fell asleep, and would sleep on until the Princess awoke and needed them. Even the fire in the kitchen fell asleep, and the castle itself.

And all this happened in an instant, for the fairies lose no time at their work.

Then the King and Queen, after kissing their dear child without causing her to stir, left the castle, and sent orders throughout the country, forbidding anyone to approach it. These orders were not necessary, for in a quarter of an hour there sprang up all round

the park such an immense number of trees, large and small, such a quantity of brambles and thorns all twisted and twined together, that neither man nor beast could have passed through them; indeed, nothing could be seen of the castle except the tops of the towers, and even they only from a great distance.

Now and again, a Prince would take the quest upon him and try to force his way through the thick hedge. But no one succeeded. The sharp thorns gripped the unhappy, young men like clutching hands, and held them fast, so that they could neither go forward nor back, and they perished miserably.

At the end of a hundred years, a new King of quite a different family was reigning in that land. One day his son happened to be hunting in the neighborhood of the sleeping castle. Seeing towers peeping above the trees in a very large wood, he asked what they were, and the country-folk told him the stories they had heard. Some said it was an old castle haunted by ghosts, others that the witches gathered there at midnight, but the most common opinion was that an ogre lived there, who ran off with all the children he could catch, to eat them at his leisure. No one could pursue him, for he alone was able to pass through the wood.

The Prince knew not what to believe.
Then an old peasant hobbled up to him.

"Your highness," he said, "More than fifty years ago I heard some one tell my father that there was a Princess in the castle—the loveliest Princess in all the world. She was bewitched and had to sleep for a hundred years. At the end of that time she would be wakened by the son of a King."

On hearing this the young Prince was much excited. He felt sure that he was the King's son who could break the spell, and he determined to see at once whether the story was true.

ARackham

No sooner did he step toward the wood than all the tall trees, the thorn hedge and the bramble-bushes parted, of their own accord, to let him pass through. He hastened toward the castle, which he saw at the end of a long avenue, and went in. He noticed with surprise that none of his people had been able to follow him, for the trees had all closed together again as soon as he had passed. But he went on without hesitation; a real Prince is always brave.

He came to a large courtyard, and all about him lay men and animals sound asleep. He crossed a court paved with marble, mounted the steps, and entered the guardroom. The sentries were drawn up in a line, with their carbines on their shoulders, but all were fast asleep. He went through several rooms full of ladies and gentlemen, all asleep, some standing, some sitting; then he came to a golden chamber, where he saw on a bed, the most beautiful sight he had ever beheld: a Princess, about sixteen, whose radiant beauty shone with almost heavenly brilliance.

The Prince drew near this lovely vision, and, in his wonder and delight, fell on his knees beside the bed. One beautiful hand lay outside the coverlet, and this he kissed gently.

Immediately the Princess' eyes flew open. "Is it you my Prince?" she said. "How long you have kept me waiting!"

Charmed with these words, and still more so by the kind and loving manner in which they were spoken, the Prince knew not how to express his joy and gratitude. He declared that he loved her more than his own life. His words were faltering and confused, but they pleased her all the more. He was much more awkward than the Princess, but this is not surprising, for she had had time to think of what she should say to him. (It is likely— though the story does not say so— that the good fairy, during this long sleep, had done her the kindness to give her pleasant dreams.) At any rate, they talked together for four hours, and even then had not said the half of the things they had to tell each other.

In the meantime, the whole palace had awakened with the Princess. Every one went about his usual task, and the lady-in-waiting came to tell the Princess that supper was served.

The Prince helped her to arise. She was magnificently dressed, but he took care not to tell

ARackham

her that she was clothed in the fashion of her great-grandmother. This, however, did not spoil her beauty in the least.

They went into a hall hung with mirrors, and there they supped, waited upon by the royal footman. The violins and oboes played tunes that were old indeed, but very pretty, though they had not been played for a hundred years.

In good time the court chaplain married the Prince and the Princess in the chapel of the castle, and who should come to bless the wedding but the same young fairy who had saved the life of the Sleeping Beauty!

What happened to the old fairy-witch I could not say, for no one ever heard of her again.